Coming Home Series

Book Two and a Half

J.M. Adele

All Titles by
J.M. Adele

Coming Home Series

Shattered Home—a Novella
Remembering Home—a Novella
Finding Home
Home Sweet Home—a Novella

Sensing Series

Sensing You
Convincing You
Indulging You

Bloodlust Series

Ashes and Dust
Ember and Flame
Bone and Blood

*Dedicated to
Cindie, Katja, and Shell.
Your unfailing friendship is life.*

Author's NOTE

Thank you for reading! *Home Sweet Home* is a companion novella to *Finding Home*, book 2 in this series. It's best to read Finding Home first. But it's okay if you don't. Each book reveals different parts of the whole story and it all comes together in the end.

If you'd prefer to read *Finding Home* first, you'll find it at jmadele.org

Enjoy!

Contents

Chapter ONE

Why Not Me?

Antonio

August 2006

Anton's eyes followed his neighbor racing by, a trail of heartbroken cries marking her path. Breadcrumbs for him to follow into the dark of night. "Lory!"

"I didn't even see her come in. Did you know she was here?" Sophia exchanged a watery wide-eyed glance with Marianne before turning to the gaping doorway.

The undeniable point of no return. The divide that had split his family, claimed his uncle years before, and would soon grant a passage of freedom to Antonio's brother. All while those who remained were left to wonder what the hell just happened.

"I'll go after her." His mama sighed, resting the stack of dirty dishes she'd collected on the table. Her shoulders sloped in defeat, betraying the magnitude of responsibility she carried as their matriarch. Or perhaps it was the burden of releasing her firstborn from under her wing. Not that she'd had a choice. Greyson would be tossing himself out soon enough, despite their father's threat to disown him if he left. He was currently upstairs packing his shit, while Anton and the feminine contingent of *la famiglia* endured the fallout.

"No, I'll go. You've got enough to deal with here." Anton's gaze darted to his father's empty seat at the head of the table before he lifted his chin towards his sisters. Marianne had her arm around her younger sibling, Sophia. Both were sniffling as they scrubbed away tears.

"Go." His mama nodded, picking up the plates, her eyes glistening with sorrow of her own.

Muscles tight with tension, Anton followed Lory's trail out of the house. He was glad his brother was finally leaving. Grey had bitched about this place for long enough. How many years had it taken him to grow the balls to do something about his misery? Yeah, Anton was happy for Grey. But any fuel feeding the positive emotion was consumed by the growing furnace of anger.

The dumb shit hadn't even considered his supposed fiancée.

Anton hoped to God Lory wasn't aiming to get behind a wheel, in her state. He upped his pace to a slow jog, a sick twist in his gut urging him on.

Everybody thought Greyson and Lorelei were the real deal. Including Lory. But Antonio knew the truth. It was all a bullshit ruse to keep everyone else happy. And it had started when Grey took it upon himself to deter Jake Johnson and every other undeserving hopeful from trying it on with the southern beauty next door. Grey came up with the plan in cahoots with Lory's brother, Clay. Lory was in on it, too. Trouble was, she had actually fallen for the Italian cowboy. And Clay had come to believe that Grey was genuinely in love with his sister, so he'd gone along with it.

What a fucking mess.

Antonio found Lory leaning against his truck, her hands covering her face as her shoulders jerked with each sob.

Where's her car? "Did you walk here?"

Her arms dropped and she raised her bloodshot stare to meet his. With a dip of her chin, she confirmed his suspicions.

"Wanna go for a drive?"

Another nod.

He opened the passenger door and guided her in, then helped her with the seatbelt. Her trembling limbs didn't seem up for any fine-motor challenges. After hot footing it to his side, he planted his butt in the driver's seat before cranking the engine. He knew better than to ask where to. With her head down and eyes locked on her clasped hands, the only place she probably wanted to go was in her imagination—where her and Greyson's life together still existed.

But what would Anton know? Maybe she was picturing being behind the wheel when Greyson emerged from the house, and her foot accidentally slamming the gas pedal to the floor. Who knew what the heck went on in females' heads? Especially when they were emotional.

Throwing the car into reverse, he backed away from the house and turned down the gravel driveway. They drove a few hundred feet before they hit the road, giving him enough time to figure out where to take her. He *could* drive aimlessly. But after a while, they'd hit the border and he'd have to turn back. Unless she was planning on getting a head start and beating Grey to Boston? If she wanted to chase him, she'd have to go it alone. Antonio wasn't having any part of that.

"I want a drink," she croaked.

He took his eyes off the road for a second. Long enough to catch her scowling at the windscreen. "I'll stop at the gas station."

"I want liquor."

His brows rose as he glanced at her again, meeting her determined stare. "Okay, then." Fixing his attention on the road, he tapped his fingers on the steering wheel, whistling a tune. A careless front to cover the internal Titanic reenactment his gut was working. At least he'd be there to keep her from doing something she'd regret. Making use of a side street to double back the way they'd come, he drove into town.

There were two places the townsfolk went to get a drink: Mama's Roadhouse and Grill, or The Beam Bar. Mama's served alcohol on the side of a mean plate of southern goodness. The Beam aimed to ply its customers with eighty-proof before sending them home with a designated driver. Or a cab. The owner had been known to confiscate keys before he'd let folks leave. And you were damned lucky if you got a handful of beer nuts to soak up the kick from the drink. O'course, the nuts came with a side of *E. coli*, so it was best to avoid them altogether.

The Beam was a bad idea. *Sooo bad*. He almost shuddered.

Yep. Mama's it is.

"And don't you dare go to Mama's."

Okaaay. Jesus. She was determined to wipe Greyson from her brain cells. *Would I get blind drunk if the love of my life walked out?* He slid his eyes sideways. *Yeah. Yeah, I would.*

Pulling into the parking lot of the bar, he stiffened on seeing Jake Johnson's red Mustang. *He* would *have to be here.* The guy went after anything with tits, but he'd taken a particular liking to Lory back in freshman year and hadn't let up. Not since Greyson and Clay made her the forbidden fruit.

"You sure you don't just wanna pick up somethin' from the liquor store, and park out in the field?"

"I'm sure." She flung open her door, and marched for the entrance, disappearing inside before Anton had a chance to turn off the engine.

Damn.

After he slid from his seat and locked the truck, he jammed his hands deep in his pockets as he approached the impending train wreck. He hoped she'd find the darkest corner to nurse a low ball, and snarl at any poor soul who tried to approach.

The bar was a little worse for wear, its neon sign long since giving up the 'h' and a 'Be', renaming the establishment T e am Bar. Local football fans claimed it was in honor of their beloved sport, but the bar culture was more indiscriminate. He'd seen a golf cart parked there once; it didn't matter what your sporting preference was. If you had any at all. The only requirement was a mutual need to get shit-faced.

Rockabilly tunes spilled from the open windows as easily as beverages poured from the tap. Clustered conversations added to the decibel barrage. Anton waited outside, scanning the windows, to assess what he was walking into. It seemed like a regular night at the bar. Piss talkin', one-uppin', and back slappin'. Anxiety yanked his hairs on end when he saw Jake leaning over a table, his body mostly covering whom he was talking to. The only visible part of his companion was long blonde hair covering one shoulder.

The same shade as Lory's.

Fuck.

Antonio wanted to march in there and pull her into the safety of his arms, assuring her everything would be okay. And to tell her that his brother was a dick for letting her go. Would she appreciate it? Nope. Would she listen? Hell no. Lory had a mind of her own.

He sighed and pinched the bridge of his nose. The odor of smoke, sweat, alcohol, and bad decisions hit him before he opened the door. Every bar smelled the same; he preferred the scent of the barn any day.

As soon as his feet crossed the threshold, his shoulders braced for a fight. *Shit.* Lory leaned over the pool table, preparing to take a shot. Her skirt rode up the backs of her thighs, giving several roving eyes a show. Including that fucker, Jake, who'd taken her vacated chair.

Anton's eyebrows lowered, and he counted to five before finding that dingy corner he'd prayed she'd be in. Catching the eye of the bartender, he held up two fingers. Viv nodded, and in less than a minute, he had two beers joining him for the shit show.

The song changed to a Keith Urban favorite, and Lory's hips began to sway. Anton downed half his beer in three gulps, hissing before clanking the glass on the sticky wooden surface.

Jake rose from his seat, and sidled up behind Lory, placing his hands over hers on the pool cue. She turned, lips pulling into a tight smile, and shouldered his chest. He raised his hands but didn't retreat the required step. Jake was a big guy at about six foot two, and two hundred plus pounds. There was no way a tiny thing like Lory could make him budge with a mere shove. But she had all the power in the world to bring a man to his knees if she wanted.

What are ya gonna do, princess?

After finishing his first beer, Anton picked up the next before leaning against the backrest of his chair. His lazy posture wouldn't have fooled anyone who truly knew him. The second Jake's hands wandered an inch too close to her skin, Anton would be on him. But, unlike Grey, Anton didn't assume she needed protecting.

Lory's hands drifted down the cue before readjusting to a firmer grip. Like she was holding a staff.

Lory's lips moved as she stared Jake in the eye. Whatever she said, he didn't like, and a sneer formed on his face. His expression quickly changed when she expertly 'passed the baton', lodging it in his groin. Levering forward, his eyes bugged out as he white-knuckled the cue.

Being mid-gulp through another mouthful, Anton barely prevented his nose from becoming a beer sprinkler. Swiping the back of his hand under his chin, he blinked. "Oh, shit. She ninja'd his ass."

Sweet Jesus, that's hot.

Twirling away from the table, Lory skipped to the jukebox by the restrooms. Her finger ran down the glass window and she tapped once before pausing. Head popping up, her eyes roamed the room, finally landing on Antonio. A sly grin tugged at her lips as she beckoned him with a crook of her finger.

Oh, damn. He ignored the way his body tightened. He was an expert at pretending she didn't rev his engine. With a shake of his head, he brought his glass to his lips once again.

I ain't chasin' you, honey.

Her smile grew wider. Both hands mimicked pulling on a rope as she sidled up to his table. "Don't ya know, you should come when a woman calls?"

He wasn't touching that comment. Caging a groan, he pulled out his wallet and handed her a fiver. "Is that what you want?"

Lory sighed with a satisfied smile. Plucking the note from his fingers, she blew him a kiss before sashaying back to choose her song. He watched her ass the whole way. As good as Anton was at resisting the urge to stare, sometimes he let himself surrender. He was pretty goddamn sick of denying his desire for her.

Lory chose her song then began to sway.

How. The. Fuck. Had his brother walked away? *Dumbass.*

Being on the receiving end of her flirtations was a first for Anton. Sure, she'd teased him before. Like a big sister teased a little brother. But this siren song was something she'd reserved solely for his older sibling.

As far as he knew.

That little mind detour had him holding in a mouthful of beer, his gaze searching every pair of eyes that tracked her movements. And there were several. Could he blame her if she'd fooled around when her supposed fiancé hadn't given her anywhere near the attention she deserved? He took another sip, the fizzy brew sliding down his throat before he pushed away the still half-full glass. He'd swallowed enough bitter-tasting truths for a lifetime.

Before long, she danced her way over to him, tugging on his hand. He tensed again. She was pulling him towards the edge of a ravine, and she had no idea.

Eyes glassy, breath smelling of tequila, she leaned down to whisper, "Dance with me."

He coughed up a laugh. She may as well have said, *'Fall with me. Die a sweet death for me.'*

In her attempt to cover her pain, she'd brought his to the surface. And she appeared to be clueless to his unrequited love.

He resisted the pull. "How much did you drink before I walked in?"

"Three shots. Why?"

"Has it gone to your head?"

"Relax. It's one dance."

Another humorless laugh caught in his throat.

No, sweetheart. It's so much more.
Having her in his arms would be like a key in a rusty lock to Pandora's box.

Chapter TWO

Memory Reel

Lorelei

It took some effort to open her eyelids a mere slit. She shut them as soon as she'd achieved the feat. Beautiful as they were, the dawn's first rays weren't so kind to her alcohol-infused retinas. Had she left the curtains open? Her usual enjoyment of the cardinals' and robins' bird song was marred by a god-awful hammering inside her cranium. How much had she drunk last night? Why could she feel a breeze?

Jostled by movement beneath her, she expelled a hiss of pain as her eyes sprang open. Lory shielded her face with her hands, peeking at her surroundings through the cracks between her fingers. Wide open Mississippi sky. This wasn't her bedroom, that was for sure. Rolling to the side, she gently pushed herself upright. A couple of blankets provided cushioning in the tray of a pickup, while another covered her legs. Poking out the bottom, a pair of boots, presumably attached to a pair of feet, announced that she had company.

Shit. Her stomach twisted. *Shit, shit, shit.*

Digging through her pickled brain, she tried to piece together the night before. Whose truck was this?

Layered over the outfit she'd worn last night, a red flannel shirt wrapped her in comfort and warmth. It kinda looked familiar. Why was she wearing a man's clothes? What the hell had she done? Consternation heated her face as her heartbeat picked up the pace. Tugging the collar to her nose, Lory drew in its beer and smoke scent. She inched her head around, to identify the garment's owner.

Oh, thank God. Antonio.

Wait... Her eyes flared as she bit her lip.

Jesus! Antonio? Really?

She ended up with her ex-fiancé's brother? Good lord, she needed to go before he woke up. *What have we done?*

He rested one hand across his stomach while the other rested above his head, near the butt of his shotgun. His bare chest rose and fell in a gentle rhythm. The crease between his brows hinted at troubled dreams. Apart from his dark stubble, he was clean-cut. Not as wild as his brother, but he was equally as beautiful.

And all at once, the night before came crashing into her awareness.

Greyson on his knees, begging her to understand. Behind him, a suitcase stuffed with the selections from this life he'd been willing to take into his new beginning. It had been as glaringly obvious as a billboard. She hadn't been on his packing list.

Her stomach roiled as the pounding in her head intensified, while tears welled in her eyes. She crept to the edge of the tray and eased herself down, landing in the freshly harvested soil. Stray pieces of straw were strewn across the earth. Searching the horizon for a landmark, she tried to figure out which field they were in. After spotting a lone Autumn Blaze maple on a hill in the distance, she knew they were on Agrioli land. With one last look at Toni, she silently thanked him for being a gentleman. Something his brother was apparently incapable of.

Whatever they'd gotten up to last night, he'd made sure she was warm and safe.

She aimed for the blushing point of color, knowing that her home wasn't too far to the west. Her sanctuary. Her escape for the next however long it took to stitch her heart back together.

———

The old screen door on the back porch creaked as she tugged it open. Coffee and freshly baked bread added their aroma to the welcoming—yellow—country kitchen. Any other day, she would've grabbed at the offerings. Her stomach reminded her today was not an average day.

"Lory? Is that you?" Her mother's voice echoed down the stairwell.

"Yeah."

"Oh, thank God." Her pajama-clad mama rushed into the room; hair haphazardly pulled into a bun. "I haven't slept a wink."

"I'm sorry. I should have called."

"No, no. Antonio let us know where you were. I could kill his brother for doing this to you."

"He told you?" Lory squeezed her eyes shut to hold back the tears as her mama drew her into an embrace.

"Antonio knew we'd worry if you didn't come home. Aw, honeypie. Grey didn't deserve you."

Lorelei dragged in air. "That's not true. He's a good man. We all knew he had dreams to chase."

But why couldn't he have taken her along for the ride?

Mama huffed. "Well, he should've gone about it with a little more care."

Yes, he should have. Lory had been discarded along with everything else he'd left behind.

Damn, it hurts.

Her mother pressed her lips into Lory's hair. "*Oof.* You smell like a brewery. Go on and get cleaned up. I'll have some breakfast waitin' for you."

"Thanks, but I don't think I can tolerate any food. I'm just gonna go to bed."

Her mother took her time before she released the hug. "Okay, baby."

Lorelei tried on a small smile and made her exit.

She reached the top of the stairs when Clay's door swung open. His face was a picture of fury if she'd ever seen one. The golden tones of his skin and hair didn't match the condemnation cloaking his tensed body. He was poised for battle, but the enemy had already retreated.

"I will hunt him down and cripple him."

She rolled her eyes. "For being true to himself?"

"Stop being a goddamn martyr." He pounded a fist on the wall.

Her shoulders sagged. "What would you have me do?"

"Get angry." He tossed his hands up. "Throw some shit."

"What's the point?"

"It'll make *me* feel better." Gripping the top of the doorjamb, he leaned into a stretch.

"Won't help me none."

"So, you're just gonna lie down and take it?"

Lowering her head, she frowned. "No. Last night, I drank myself into oblivion. Now I'm gonna catch up on sleep. And later, I'll probably cry some more."

Clay let his arms hang loose by his sides. "Sounds like you have it all figured out."

"I got the next twenty-four hours sorted." She held up her left thumb and gave a mock smile.

Shards of light glinted off her diamond ring, drawing forth a tide of emotions. Lory slammed her eyes shut and dropped her hand. Her thumb found its way to the metal band, twisting it around her finger. *I can't take it off. Not yet.*

"I'm still gonna hurt him. Enjoy your hangover." He gave her a pat on the back as he headed for the stairs.

She shook her head, turning to face her door. Her breath caught as she entered the room. The four walls surrounded her in memories of *him*. Pictures, gifts they'd exchanged, words both spoken and unspoken bulldozing her thoughts. She wanted to stuff them all in a trash bag and toss it in the bottom of her closet. Discard him like he'd done to her. Or maybe she could bolt for the safety of… where? Every corner of their land held fragments of a time they'd had together. She'd have to leave town to have any chance of wiping him out altogether. And even then, he was still in her heart, damn it. She couldn't rip it out of her chest and throw it in the back of his pickup yelling, 'Hey! You forgot something.' The only thing she *could* do was down some painkillers and collapse on the bed, letting the memory reel flatten her to nothing.

This was her fault. She'd known it wasn't solid from the start.

Eight years ago. Way back in freshman year…

"We spend so much time together; people think we're dating." Lory *put the statement out there, half hoping he'd tell her she was his one and only.*

"Let 'em think what they want. If it keeps the assholes away from you, what would be the harm?"

"Right. I guess." It wasn't exactly the answer she'd anticipated.

"So, we are *dating?"*

He hooked his arm around her shoulders and kissed her temple. "That okay with you?"

It had been more than fine. A dream come true.

Inside her chest, echoes of the euphoria she'd experienced at the time tried to flicker to life.

But it had been just a fantasy.

A chimera.

A castle built on quicksand, destined to crumble.

Why *had* he asked her to marry him?

The answer struck with painful clarity. Because it was a natural progression. The payoff for all the years invested. But their engagement had been more about giving in to everyone's expectations—including hers—and less about Grey seeing a life with her. Lorelei sensed Grey hadn't been all in, even if she'd fallen.

Hard.

Was it his problem that somewhere along the way she'd developed real feelings, while he'd kept her in the friend zone?

What an idiot I've been.

Her nose curled. With the pain killers working their magic, she became acutely aware of the bar stench rising from her clothes and hair. She slowly sat up before tugging Toni's shirt off.

I should thank him.

There was no way she could face him today, though. Or anytime soon. And she didn't want to know what happened in the back of his truck.

Grabbing her phone, she typed out a quick text.

Hey. Thanks for getting me home safely. I'll see you around sometime.

Waaay down the track.

She switched off her phone and tossed it on the nightstand.

It was best to stay away from Agriolis altogether.

Chapter
THREE

Ready When You Are

Antonio

Three Weeks Later

Anton tightened the last two bolts to fix the snorkel on the tractor, the final piece replaced after changing a broken fan belt. Giving it a jiggle, he made sure it was secure. With a nod to Papà, he took a step back as he wiped his hands on a rag. "Okay, turn her over."

The engine roared to life, the smell of diesel cloying the air in the equipment shed. The corrugated iron structure housed their two tractors, along with the various attachments they used for maintaining their crops. Three walls were lined with hooks and shelves that were loaded with parts, containers, hoses, ropes, and all sorts of essential tools of the trade. Whatever they needed for maintenance, it was either in this shed, or its neighbor that held the four-wheelers. Two roller doors opened to a view of the paddock, which was behind the farmhouse. In the distance, the sheets on the line flapped in the breeze like a flag on a hill. Anton's stomach rumbled; it would be time for breakfast soon.

"Bravo." His papà clapped his hands before rubbing them together. "Let's see the chef do that." He turned off the engine and hopped down.

Anton shook his head. "Grey knows his way around an engine."

"I wasn't referring to your brother."

"Uncle Matteo?"

Papà ground his teeth together before mumbling an Italian curse that Anton had only heard once before. When an eight-year-old Sophia had taken his truck for an ill-fated joyride. Thankfully, the only casualty had been the chicken coop.

Uncle Matteo hadn't set foot on the family property for twenty-five years. Nonno had died without speaking to his eldest son again, and the rift between the brothers continued to this day.

"What happened for you to hate him so much? Why did Nonno cast him out?"

"Nothing."

"You can't keep—"

His papà sliced a hand through the air. "*Basta*! It's nothing to do with you."

"Ah, that's where you're wrong. It has affected my entire life. And now it's impacting others."

"Who?" Papà snapped.

"The Carters. Lory." Anton hadn't seen her since the bar.

Papà scoffed. "The moment you lose your heart to a woman, you are ruined. And you will hurt everyone around you, to have her for yourself. But perhaps it is too late for you?"

Anton scowled to cover the sick feeling rising in his gut. Had his secret been exposed? "What?"

"*Non fare lo stupido.* I see it all over your face."

'Don't be stupid.' Papà's words echoed in his head. Anton reared back as he threw the greasy rag in a bucket. "You're wrong."

Papà laughed. "Am I?"

"Yes." Anton clenched his jaw. It took a lot to get him riled up, but his father had found his weak spot.

"A father knows his son. One day you will understand."

"Is that right? Then why were you so surprised when Grey told you he was leavin'?" Anton cocked a brow, half disbelieving that he was confronting the old man, and half revved for a fight.

His father bared his teeth, spitting out a string of curses. "*Sei una tale merda.* You dare to challenge me? I know what's best for my children. He will be back."

Is calling your child a shit what's best, Papà?

"I thought he wasn't welcome," Anton spat.

His father's mouth snapped shut, rage twisting his features into gnarled lines. "Pack up the trailer with the gear for the State Fair. Tomorrow, you'll prepare the stalls for our arrival next week."

Anton nodded.

"You will go in place of your brother. It's Sophia's last year showing the cattle. Don't ruin it for her."

"*Sì.*"

Papà climbed on the tractor, leaving Anton behind without another word. They'd probably ignore each other for a week.

Turning away, he hung his head. "Fuck." He raised his arms, ready to dive his hands through his hair before remembering they were filthy. "Fuuuuuck." The word roared from his mouth. His body was strung so tight he could've crushed rocks in his palms. *Damn.* He needed to let off steam. He'd been so busy with the last few newborn calves of the season that he'd barely slept in weeks. Three, to be exact. Not since he'd drifted off under the stars with Lory's body curled against his.

Goddamn it.

"Toni?"

Oh, great. Now I'm hearing her voice. He released a groan of frustration as he scrubbed his greasy fingers over his cropped hair. *Fuck it. It'll wash out.*

"Are you growlin' at me?"

Spinning around, he found Lory standing in the doorway.

Jesus! Of all the times to show up.

"Hey." Anton grabbed his hat in the hopes it would shield her eyes from the red rising in his cheeks.

"Hi. Your mama said I'd find you here." She hooked her thumbs in the pockets of her jeans and came closer.

Seeing her again was like the first ice-cold drink after a day of working in the field.

"I didn't mean to overhear."

Oh, shit. Which part had she heard? "Uh—"

"You're setting up the stalls tomorrow?"

Thank Christ. "Yeah."

"I didn't realize it was Sophia's last year, but I guess she's eighteen now. I think Mama wishes I was still showing the cattle. She wants me out of the house. I've scrubbed every surface twice and cleaned out every cupboard. I might've thrown out some things I shouldn't have."

"Is that right?" Lord, she was beautiful, even when she babbled.

"I didn't know the tin of cocoa wasn't what it advertised on the label. It was twenty years out of date."

He raised a brow. "What was in it?"

"Some old love letters Daddy wrote her when they started datin'."

"Did you get them out of the trash in time?"

"Yeah. But I've been banned from unsupervised cleaning."

She was fucking adorable. Anton couldn't stop the grin even if he wanted to.

"Are you busy?" she asked.

I wish I wasn't. "I've gotta go check on the weanlings in the northeast paddock."

She nodded, then dropped her gaze to the ground. "Okay."

Damn, she sounded so sad. Lonely, maybe. And lord knew he didn't want to leave her behind. "Wanna come?"

Her chin lifted as her grin spread. "Okay."

When she smiled, really smiled, there was the faintest hint of a dimple in her left cheek. The fact that he'd made it appear after all she'd been through made him feel ten feet tall. If he had one mission in life, it was to make her do that every day.

Anton led her to the shed where they kept the four-wheelers and took the driver's seat, cranking the motor. In the distance, he saw Dodger bounding towards them. The sound of the engine was like a dinner bell for their Border Collie. He came running every time.

Lory settled in place behind Anton just as Dodger jumped on his lap, licking his face.

"Ugh, Dodge!"

He wiped the slobber on his shoulder, pausing as Lory's chest pressed against his back, her giggles vibrating through his ribcage. Her hands were clutched at his sides, her thighs pressed against the back of his. Anton's body clenched for an entirely different reason than before.

He pressed his lips together, exhaling slowly before swallowing. Twisting his head, he caught her in his peripheral, noting that her beautiful smile was still in place. "You ready?"

"When you are," she replied.

If only that were true, sweetheart.

Chapter FOUR

Confined Spaces

Lorelei

Antonio pulled the vehicle to a stop just inside the gate. She released her grip around his waist and hopped off to open the way. Dodger jumped down, black and white fur bouncing as he ran around the cattle.

Anton drove a short way up the hill to park on level ground, the group of newly weaned spring calves dispersing around him. Some bellowed at the intrusion before sniffing at the fence to find their mothers grazing on the other side. Others ignored him altogether, going back to their tasty patch of pasture.

Lory secured the latch before making her way on shaky legs to meet him on the crest of the rise. He struck an imposing figure, standing tall at the top, overlooking the land. Yeah, he was a lot like Grey. And that was where things got a little blurred. She'd liked the feel of his body against hers a little too much. Her stomach fluttered at the thought. *Stop it*. But was it only because she was lonely and missing his brother?

No.

She was both of those things, but deep down, she'd spent years keeping Toni at arm's length because she wasn't entirely unaffected by his presence. But she loved Grey. She'd always wanted Greyson. Hadn't she?

"I never properly thanked you." Her voice croaked as she broached the reason why she'd come to find him.

"For what?"

"For takin' care of me at the bar. You know… *that* night."

"No need. I'm here for you anytime."

"You don't have to be polite. I was a hothouse mess. I just don't want things to be weird between us."

"I'm sure we'll manage. It's not the first time I've seen another side of you."

"What do you mean?"

"Remember when I found you hangin' by your shoe from a tree with your dress around your neck?"

Shoulders dropping, she tilted her head and stared at him, unimpressed. "I was eight."

"I was nine. I'll never forget it." One cheek pulled up in a lopsided grin as his gaze focused on her neck. Probably watching the flush of heat taking over.

She retaliated with a cringeworthy moment from the Antonio vault. "I remember the first time you got drunk. I found you under the bleachers, hurlin' your dinner." Oh, yeah. He'd been smashed.

He shrugged like it had been nothing. "A senior's rite of passage. And besides, you did the same thing the next year."

God, she'd forgotten about that. "True. We have way too much dirt on each other."

"Your secrets are safe with me."

A small smile graced her lips because she knew he spoke the truth.

His gaze darted away, but not before she noted the shadows under his eyes. "How are you doing? I lost a fiancé, but you lost a brother."

He grabbed a handful of dirt, rubbing it through his fingers. "I didn't lose him. He's just elsewhere, tryna find his purpose. I'm lucky I've always known my calling. Not a lot of people can say that at twenty-four."

"Yeah. I guess you're right."

"Do you think he'll ever come back?" Her throat squeezed around the question.

"In time, maybe. Papà needs to find it in his heart to forgive him before he'll let Grey set foot on the property again."

Dodger sniffed around his heels before sitting on Anton's feet. He leaned down to scratch his faithful companion behind the ears.

Lory crouched to give the dog a pat, and he rolled over, pawing the air as if asking for a belly rub. She obliged.

"What about you? Have you found your purpose yet?"

She twisted her neck to take him in, squinting one eye shut against the bright sun. "I love farm life. I've never wanted anythin' else. I've thought about studying agriculture. I'd be more help around the farm if I were up on all the latest technology and research. But Mississippi State is two hours away. Too far to travel on the regular. I'd have to move."

"I guess we have more in common than we thought."

"You want to study?"

He dipped his chin. "I'm hoping to start next year. If Papà didn't need me around here as much, I'd be learnin' full-time. And now that we're a ranch hand down… well, I guess I'll have to wait a bit longer."

"Maybe if your father gets more help, we could be roomies?"

His chest rose before he huffed a laugh and shook his head.

Right. Bad idea, obviously.

She needed to get away from the Agrioli men altogether.

Antonio

Sharing a confined space with the unattainable object of his desire—that equaled hell in his book. It was bad enough having her this close and pretending he didn't want to kiss the lovin' hell out of her. Why would he do it to himself?

In any case, a relationship needed two things to work: chemistry and compatibility. They had the latter—of that he was certain. But when it came to the former, Anton was all on his own. Unrequited love was a collar wrapped around his neck—a constant pressure threatening to cut off his oxygen supply.

"Uh, I gotta check the fences while I'm here. Some of the calves can be overzealous when they're lookin' for their mamas." He turned and walked along the slatted wood fences dividing the paddocks that he'd already checked before bringing the weanlings up.

"Oh, I know. Poor babies. It's awful separating the pairs. I don't like those nasty lookin' spiked nose rings Daddy uses to wean the calves though. It might keep the pairs together, but it hurts the cows when the babies try to suckle. I keep tellin' him."

"I guess he has to choose the method that he feels is right." Anton quickened his pace, praying for the torment to be over.

"True." She trotted to catch up. "I wanted to ask about the night at the bar. I don't remember much after my third shot of tequila, but I do remember earlier on. I saw your face when you were walkin' to the table. You were angry about somethin'. I'm sorry if I dragged you into a situation you didn't wanna be a part of."

He stopped and turned to face her. "It wasn't that."

"Then what was it?" She raised her brows.

Anton's jaw clenched. He forced his teeth apart so he could speak. "I didn't like the way Jake was lookin' at you."

"But you didn't save me when he made a move. Your brother wouldn't have let him breathe on me; why didn't you come over?"

Anton's mouth tightened at the comparison between him and Greyson. "You had it under control.

It was good for Jake to see that you could hold your own."

She looked lost in thought for a second before her spine straightened. "You're right. And I'd be lying if I didn't say it was liberating to stand up for myself."

Spinning away, he scanned the contours of the land to remind himself he had all the space in the world. So why did he feel cornered?

Lory stepped up beside him, folding her arms around her middle. "How could anyone not appreciate this?"

"I got no idea. Maybe you need to ask Grey." He spoke through gritted teeth, praying for patience. She was working out her grief. Trying to understand where things had gone wrong. He got that. But it took all Anton's strength not to curse his brother's name and tell her she'd fallen for the wrong Agrioli.

"You're not in the mood to talk, are you?"

"I'll talk about anythin' but him."

Her shoulders rose as she gripped each elbow. "I'm sorry. I've been insensitive. This is hard for you, too."

Anton groaned. He was the insensitive one. He'd never seen her look so lost. So vulnerable. Reaching over, he pulled her into his arms and rested his chin on her hair. "You're gonna be okay. Maybe things didn't work out how you thought they would, but you got good things comin'. And they'll be better than you imagined."

She had to—a person as selfless and strong as her deserved the world.

Her tentative touch brushed his back. "I hope so," she returned, her voice barely more than a whisper. "Thank you."

"Anythin' for you."

Everything.

Even confined spaces.

Damn it.

Chapter FIVE

Fair's Fair

Antonio

October

The whir of the blow-dryer was deafening as Anton dried Betsy off after her first wash of the day. Floating strands of red and white Hereford hair caught on his skin and teased his nostrils. Their steer, Waldo, was already clean. He was waiting for Betsy to be tethered beside him so they could have breakfast. Farther down the barn, similar scenes played out. The buzz before judging was gaining momentum.

Waldo mooed while batting his lashes at Marianne.

"It's coming, baby. I know you're hungry." She measured the oats, corn, and protein into the feeders for the two head of cattle.

He switched the dryer off just as Sophia came in.

"How do I look?" She tugged on her harness with one hand and held her show stick in the other.

She looked the part with her blue button up, jeans with concho belt, and cowgirl boots and hat to match. The younger of his sisters was so much like their Nonna with her dark hair and eyes. She had the temper to match, too. Marianne was more like Mama. Softer spoken, lighter in features. They both worked just as hard as each other, making a good team. Whereas, in contrast, Grey and Anton had sometimes been at odds. Mainly because Grey hated cow shit and hay baling.

"Ready." He nodded once.

"Number seventeen-seventeen. That's gotta be lucky, right?" She patted the number on her harness.

"I reckon so."

His eyes strayed for the fiftieth time to the stalls across from them. Lorelei and Clay were making their way around, saying hello to the other exhibitors. He paid the others no mind, his focus half on his job and half on Lory. She wore a similar getup to Sophia, but without the hat, and her shirt had western-style checks. Her jeans fit her just right.

A tap on his arm dragged his attention back to his sister.

"What?"

Sophia wore a troubled expression, a crease marring her brow. "I said, are ya done with Betsy? They need to eat."

"Yeah, sure. I'll brush her down after."

"I'll brush her down. You go on over and talk to Clay and Lory instead of standing there staring. It's creeping me out." She pushed him aside, resting the show stick on the stall wall.

Sophia grabbed the brush and went about taming the Hereford's hair.

Shoulders bunched; Anton hesitated to turn around. Why did he feel like the ground beneath him was about to give way? He'd always known where he stood with Lory. He was a friend. He was her boyfriend's brother. But now that Grey was out of the picture it seemed like Anton and Lory's parallel paths were converging. The roadblocks were gone, but so were the street signs. He didn't know how to navigate his way to safety. If he spoke to her, spent more time with her, he'd fall deeper in love. And that only meant pain. It was better to avoid her. At all costs. She'd probably think he was an asshole, but better that than a pathetic dick.

He went to grab the other brush, but Sophia sidestepped to block his path. "What are ya doin'?"

"I'm helpin' you. What's your problem?"

With a deliberate glance and chin lift towards the opposite stall, she repeated her question. "What. Are. You. Doing?"

His gut sank.

Why the fuck couldn't he control himself when Lory was near? "Nothin'."

Sophia raised her eyebrows, exchanging a glance with Marianne who wore an identical look of disbelief. "It doesn't look like nothin'. Did somethin' happen between you and Lory? 'Cause she's been sneakin' glances over here as much as you've been reciprocatin'."

Reciprocating. Yeah, right.

"Don't go makin' up stories in your head. You don't know squat." *Bury the truth in denial and fertilize it with a smile.* He'd been doing it for years.

"You're makin' it *so* obvious."

Shit… fuck… shitfuck.

"I feel bad for her. That's all." *Half-truth. Half-lie.* What did it matter anymore? He'd never have her.

"I've lived with you for eighteen years, I know when you're lying through your teeth. You got it bad. How long? Does Grey know about this?"

Anger seized his tongue. *I ain't tellin' you shit, sister.* He spun away and untied Betsy, leading her next to the steer.

Marianne averted her eyes as she distributed the feeders to the cattle. Waldo heaved himself up so he could chow down on the good stuff, while their heifer did the same.

Sophia crossed her arms and locked Anton in a stare before she marched over to their neighbors.

He almost hooked a finger in the back of her harness to yank her back.

She wouldn't dare say anything. Would she?

He started to clean up the wash station, with one eye watching his sister's arms flail as her gums flapped some undoubtedly useless information to the Carters.

What the hell are you telling them?

Sophia spun back to him with a big grin. "I'll see you in the arena, Lory," she called over her shoulder. Bypassing Anton, she gave Marianne's arm a squeeze. "I'm off the find Mama and Papà." And then she was gone, leaving him with a lump of sick in the back of his throat.

Twisting around, he caught Lory's eyes just before they darted back to her brother.

The hell?

He desperately swallowed, almost choking. *Fuck.* Sophia was a master meddler.

Whatever she'd done, it couldn't be good.

Marianne dusted off her hands before propping them on her hips. "I'm going to get ready. You okay to help Soph finish up the beauty routine?"

"Yeah, go do whatcha gotta do."

She took off, and he found his mind straying where it shouldn't go once more. His eyes followed, but Lory was gone.

It was for the best. He was acting like a lovesick fool. If there was an antidote to his obsession, he needed it bad. Whatever it took to make his daydreams shrivel up and die. He wanted out of this mental prison.

What else could he do?

"You okay there, champ?" Clay called out, pausing his conversation with Sophia's competition.

Fuck, no. "Yup, all good."

"Catch up tonight?"

"Sure thing."

Maybe getting drunk with her brother was an excellent idea.

Or maybe he'd confess his love in his alcoholic stupor. Then just about everybody would know his feelings except the object of his affection.

Yeah, probably not a good plan.

―――

Holding his hat to his chest, Antonio moved through the crowds in the judging arena. The stands surrounding the ring were mostly filled with excited family members and friends. He'd been to enough of these things to recognize many faces. He said his hellos and managed to keep moving without getting pulled into small-talk hell. On the far side, he caught sight of his papà talking to members of the Cattlemen's Association. Scanning the bleachers, he found his mama wearing her Agrioli Farms shirt. He too was flying the flag with his green tee sporting a red bull, and their name emblazoned in white writing. Another two minutes of 'Excuse me's' and 'Hey, how are ya's?' and he'd finally reached her.

"Hey. Thanks for saving me a seat." Anton took his place beside her as the heifers were led into the ring. Sophia was the last to enter.

"That's okay, honey. You missed the steer show."

"I know. Sorry. I was…" *Getting my head in gear* "…cleaning."

"Did you see Lory and Clay? They're over the other side with their daddy." She pointed across the ring.

I see her. Her face haunted his dreams and his every waking thought. Just like a declaration of love carved into a hundred-year-old tree, there was no erasing it. Her mark grew with him, becoming callus with time.

"Lorelei seems to be doing okay. Have you spoken to her much?"

In the flesh? Not nearly enough. "Nah. She's been quiet."

"I don't blame her." Something in his mother's voice had him turning his head towards her.

She stared at the spectacle rather than him as she spoke, "How are you holdin' up?"

"I'm doin' fine." He tracked Betsy's path around the ring, figuring his mother had the right idea. If he looked at her, she'd see too much. She was perceptive like that. Try as he might to keep his focus on the heifers, he didn't last long. Guided by some magnetic force, his eyes drifted across the arena to find Lory leaning across Clay to shake someone's hand.

Goddamn it. Get out of my head.

"I know this has been tough on you too. It hurt your papà when Matteo left so abruptly. Brothers have a special bond."

"It doesn't bother me none." Another half-truth. He did miss his brother. Anton shrugged, glancing at his mom and almost doing a double take at finding her teared up. Great. Now he felt like a schmuck. Tucking her under his arm, he murmured, "Hey, I'm sure he's okay. Uncle Matteo will look after him."

She chewed her cheek, jerking her chin in a shaky nod. "I need to see him."

"Greyson? How are you gonna explain that one to Papà?"

"He cannot stop me from seeing our son. Your father may have disowned him, but I haven't. I need to see Matteo. I need to make this right."

Matteo? Wait, what? "Make what right? It was Grey's choice to leave."

"You don't understand."

"What is there to figure out?"

"Now isn't the time." She clamped her mouth shut before wiping her eyes on her sleeves.

What the hell is going on?

A quarter of a century of secrets was a heavy thing. And Grey's revolt had made them heavier. Whatever *they* were.

"I know the bulk of the work has fallen on your shoulders. Things will quieten down slightly over winter. We just have to get through the next month or so."

"I know." Anton shrugged.

"You've been so tense lately. I thought it was weighing on you, that's all."

She seemed to be the only one who didn't know about his infatuation with Grey's fiancée. *Ex* fiancée. At least he now knew that Papà and his sisters hadn't blabbed. "You know I don't like comin' to the fair. I'd rather be home." *Screw it. I'm stickin' with the denial angle.*

"Oh, honey, I'm the same. But we have to do our bit." She shuffled back in her seat. "Lory seems to like it."

He almost groaned. *Why'd you have to mention her name?* "She's good at puttin' on a brave face."

"You think?"

Oh, yeah. He nodded, watching the woman in question as she chatted with Clay.

"That's something us southern girls learn how to do at an early age." Mama's lips quivered, not quite reaching smile status. "If you don't mind, I'm going to have a little lie down in the RV. The excitement is getting to me, I think. I'll see you after."

"Okay." He frowned at her back as she jostled through the crowd.

Family secrets never stayed hidden forever. There was always something or someone that dragged them into the light. But maybe that was what she was planning to do.

He turned back, finding Lory's eyes on him as she bit her lip.

And this time, she didn't look away.

He exhaled in a rush.

A whisper of something crossed her face. Her lip popped free as she parted her lips as if to set free some secrets of her own. It was a double punch—one to the heart and one to his gut.

Sweet, sweet agony.

Chapter SIX

Giant Stuffed Unicorns

Antonio

After helping his father tuck the animals in for the night, Anton had a shower and made his way to the RV. Thankfully, Clay had bailed after finding a brunette from Jackson to pass the time with. Anton's dream of kicking back with his feet up and enjoying some alone time might have been out of reach, but he was gonna damn well try. Pulling aside the canvas, he entered the annex and dumped his dirty clothes near his swag. "It's me." He knocked on the door.

His mama opened the way. "Come on in."

The interior was spacious enough, with his parents' bedroom down one end, a small wash closet in the middle, and the kitchen/ living area near the entrance. On the front wall, a fold-down bunk provided a sleeping space for Marianne. The table could be lowered, and with the addition of some cushions from the seats, transformed into another bunk for Sophia. He had the annex all to himself. *Thank you, Grey.*

A TV sat on the kitchen bench, broadcasting the local news. Mama reached behind her to shut the dining room curtains, only partially blocking the lights from the fairgrounds. "Y'all did some real hard work these last few days. Thank you."

"We did awesome! Betsy and Waldo are stars." Marianne held a novel as she lounged on her bunk, gaze fixed on the TV.

Anton smirked. "Good book?"

"Huh?" She twisted her head, blinking at her copy of *Pride and Prejudice*, almost surprised to find the thing in her hand.

"I knew Betsy would take the prize… but poor Waldo." Sophia's bottom lip pouted as she snuggled into their mother's side on the bench.

"Fourth is a respectable placing," Mama quipped.

I guarantee Waldo doesn't give a shit about ribbons. Anton grabbed a Coke from the RV's fridge. Taking a sip, he narrowed his eyes at his mama and sisters. It was Saturday night. They were at the fair. All three of them were in their pajamas, ready for bed at six. He couldn't recall that ever happening in all the years they'd been coming. *Huh. Weird.*

"Is Papà still with the animals?"

"Yep. You know he doesn't like to leave them alone."

Anton reckoned Papà was itchin' to get them back to the farm. "Have we checked in on Dave?"

"Papà spoke to him before. Everything is fine at home. We're lucky to have the extra help. I think we need to employ him for the busy seasons, at least. Then maybe you can get your degree."

He flattened his mouth with a solemn nod. There wasn't any point in getting his hopes up for something that might never happen. Just like with Lory. It was always best to pay no mind to unattainable things. Desperation often pushed the good stuff away, in his experience. The problem was, he couldn't get her out of his head, no matter how hard he tried.

"Do you want to watch some TV with us?" Marianne asked, abandoning her novel—and all pretense of loving the classic—on the bed.

God, no. He'd spent way too much time with his sisters over the last few days. The fair was the only chance they had at a family holiday every year, but he'd prefer to continue working. "I'm just gonna chill in the annex." At least he didn't have to sleep inside with them. Although it wasn't much of a separation, being just outside in a flimsy material add-on. But, hey, he had his own TV. *Score.*

"What about dinner?" His mama frowned.

"I'll grab somethin' later."

He turned and opened the door, rearing back at finding Lory on the other side.

"Oh, hey." She blushed, tucking her hair behind her ear.

Her proximity had his body lighting up like the midway. The door handle creaked as he tightened his grip.

He cleared his throat. "Evenin'. Are you after one of the girls?"

"Hi. Yes. Sophia?"

He stepped back so she could come in.

Sophia sat up. "Lory! You came."

She hesitated in the entrance, clasping her hands. "Are you in your pajamas?"

"I'm so sorry, I should have called. I'm not feeling up to riding the roller-coaster tonight, but Antonio said he'd be happy to take you."

His jaw unhinged, and in his peripheral vision, he saw Lorelei's head swivel in his direction. Sophia angled her chin giving him a sweet smile while fluttering her lashes. His eyes narrowed. *Payback is gonna be a bitch, little sister.*

"Oh, um… only if you're sure?" Lory's brow crinkled as she bit her lip.

Christ, Sophia. What the hell? "I'd be happy to take you, if you'd like?"

She looked anything but sure as she twisted her fingers together, blinking up at him. "Okay."

Okay? Was she agreeing because she didn't want to seem rude? "I'll just grab my jacket and boots." He indicated for her to leave first.

The moment her back was turned, he glared at his grinning sister. Anton sliced a finger across his throat before turning to follow Lory, his mother's gasp chasing his retreating back.

He had to school his features before addressing Lory. "Sorry, I'll just be a sec." Reaching for his boots and jacket, he donned them like they were some sort of personal protective equipment that would shield him from her charms. An impossible feat, considering she was under his skin.

He walked her through the campground towards the midway. "Are you sure you wanna do this? I'm sorry Sophia bailed on you." *Conniving little cow.*

"We both know she didn't." Lory gave him a skeptical smile.

He should've known she'd see right through the act.

Does she see right through me?

Kids, high on cotton candy, darted around them in a game of tag, one losing part of his pink, fluffy treat to the pavement.

"You're aware of her manipulative side, huh?" Anton's eyes followed a clown on stilts as she ambled by.

Coming to a crossroad, Lory slowed for a horse being led towards the stables. "We got played. Why she dragged you into it, I don't know. Listen, if ya don't wanna hang with me, I'll be fine."

"There's nothing I'd rather do than spend time with you." The response skimmed off his tongue as easily as water.

What the hell was in that Coke? Truth serum?

They both stopped walking. Her head snapped around, gaze searching his face. He smiled and shrugged. It was too late to put the words back. She could do with them whatever she wanted. Maybe she would dump him and run.

Please stay.

He held his breath, waiting.

Lory dropped her chin, hiding her face from him.

Fuck. This was a bad idea. His mouth went dry as his gut hollowed out.

Looking up through her lashes, she asked, "What would you like to do first?"

He exhaled with a force, wanting to gather her in his arms, but he was frozen in shock. It took his brain way too long to form an answer. "Rides first. Then food. Then midway."

She smiled, her dimple making an appearance. "It's the most logical order."

"I think so. I don't wanna be riding the Mega Drop with a belly full of food while carrying a giant unicorn."

"Exactly." She laughed. "Can you guarantee an oversized stuffed toy?"

"I never miss a shot."

"Let's do this." She hooked her hand on his elbow, leading him forward.

It was official. Sophia was his favorite sister.

Chapter
SEVEN

Screamer

Lorelei

She hadn't had so much fun in what seemed like forever. Life had become an endless loop of rising with the sun, doing her chores, caring for everybody else but herself, and then going to bed. When was it her turn to live a little?

Now. Now it was her turn. What she was starting to realize was that *now* had always been the answer. Every day presented at least one moment where she could find something to treasure just for her.

She sounded like a banshee as the roller-coaster took another plunge before twisting into a loop. Gripping the rail for dear life, exhilaration collided with pure joy to split her face in a wide smile. The coaster pulled to a sudden stop, creeping forward the last few feet to let the passengers off.

She turned to find Toni grinning at her. "You're a screamer."

Her face was probably already pink from the ride. Enough to hide her responding blush. "I can't help it. There's something wrong with people who don't scream when they're hurtling through space, strapped down by a metal bar."

"What are you tryna say?" He hopped out before spinning around to help her.

"You're not normal." Her tiny hand rested in his. She didn't pull away after regaining her feet. It was too good. Sturdy. Warm.

"What is normal, anyways?" He didn't release his hold, either.

That one move spoke of possibilities. She quashed the spark of hope flickering to life. This was Toni. He was her friend.

"It's something the media made up to keep us all feeling inadequate," She quipped.

"Ooh, are we talkin' conspiracy theories?" He bumped her with his shoulder.

"I'm open if you are." She shrugged.

Could I be open to taking a leap of faith?

Flashing lights illuminated his face like the indicator on a car. Maybe they were taking a change in direction. Maybe the line between friend/neighbor and something more was getting a little blurred. As she heard the rollercoaster take a dive, dragging screams from its riders' lungs she kinda felt like she was still strapped in that seat.

What if they did start something?

If their lives collided and their potential unleashed, would it be enough to obliterate any obstacles in their way?

She had no idea. But maybe she couldn't let go of the cowboy next door that easily.

"Do aliens exist?" he asked.

She almost laughed. Not at his question, but at the realization he could be just as weird as she was. "It's a big universe. I think it'd be pretty incredible if they didn't."

He waved a hand at the sky. "What if there are multiple universes?"

"Sure. Why not?" She winked.

He tossed an arm over her shoulders. "You're a glass-half-full kinda gal."

She had to inhale to steady her rioting heart, cinnamon and sugar-coated air saturating her lungs. The blaring music, strobing lights, bustle and rabble of the crowd all faded to a din as her focus pinpointed everywhere they touched. "Just trying to see all angles."

"I wish I could be more like you." Regret edged his tone.

"Why? What's so bad about being you?"

His lips drew tight as he pushed air through his nostrils. "I've always been second best, I guess."

Surprise lifted her brows. How could he honestly believe that when he was the one his parents relied on the most? They knew he was the dependable one because the farm was more than just a job to him. "You've got middle-child syndrome."

"Is that so?" He eyed her side-on.

"Yeah. Do you remember when we were down at the river, and you caught the biggest fish, but Grey caught the most?"

"Yeah," he almost snarled.

"Your mama was so proud of both of you. She cooked a big dinner and said something about us having enough to go around. Your face dropped. You thought she was making a big deal of your brother catching more than you."

"Wasn't she?" He slowed his pace.

"Not at all. The complement was directed towards the biggest catch of the day. She was looking at you, but you were too busy scowling at your plate." And Grey had rolled his eyes like he didn't give a shit. She remembered it, plain as day.

Toni pressed his lips together, staring at his feet as they walked through the crowds.

Oh, crap. He'd gone quiet. "I've upset you."

"You've got me re-evaluating my entire childhood."

Wow. "Seriously?" She hoped that was a good thing.

"Mm-hmm."

Searching his face, she saw the boy he once was. A tender protectiveness welled behind her sternum. "You always were the deepest thinker."

"That doesn't sound like a compliment." He smirked.

"It is. It means you care. You have compassion. You don't jump into things easily." She'd always believed that the woman who got to share a life with him would be incredibly lucky. And as the thought resurfaced, this time it came with a pang of jealousy. *Crap.*

"Neither do you." He stopped in front of the giant wheel, his arm retreating from her shoulders so he could twine his fingers with hers. "Wanna see the universe?"

Lory flashed her teeth. "Which one?"

"Very funny." Tugging on her hand, he led her to the end of the queue.

The wheel turned slowly, each of its spokes decorated in lights. Ahead of them, the line-up consisted mostly of loved-up pairs. She supposed they would look like a couple to anyone who didn't know them. She'd stood there with Greyson once or twice over the years. This time it felt new. Exciting. And, if she thought about it too much, wrong. *Toni is Grey's brother, for Christ's sake. What am I doing?*

A squeeze of his grip had her lifting her chin.

"Where'd ya go?" Brows pinched together; his steel-colored eyes trained on hers.

"Nowhere. It's just a bit strange. Being here with you."

"Do you want to leave?" His tone was gruff.

"No." The word spilled out before she could think. Guilty as she was, she didn't want the night to end.

Toni scanned the crowd. "It's okay to enjoy yourself without him, you know?"

"I know." Logically, she knew. But loyalty was a hard thing to break. Even when the intended recipient was undeserving.

He dropped her hand, his own retreating into his pockets. "I don't expect anything from you. I just want you to have a good time."

"I *am* having fun." *Too much. It's too easy with you, Antonio.*

He showed their ride passes at the ticket booth before they were ushered into a gondola, each of them taking opposing sides. The wheel inched around to let each group on, swinging Lory and Toni every time. They avoided eye contact through the painfully slow process. Cheesy carnival music serenaded their awkward exchange. The distant screams of adrenaline junkies sliced through the air. Lory shivered as a cool breeze curled around her body.

Toni switched his position to sit beside her, placing his arm around her back. "I like seeing the people from up here. It reminds me how small we really are. Puts things into perspective."

She snuggled into his side. Purely for his warmth. *Liar.* She wanted to be closer to him. God, he felt so good. "See? Deep thinker."

"I'd rather be a deep thinker than a screamer."

"Hey!" She tried to sit forward, but he pulled her into his chest, and kissed the top of her head.

Tingles flooded her body as her heart kicked. "Did you just—"

"Do you think a screamer could ever love a deep thinker?" His mouth was so close to her ear, she heard him loud and clear.

Lory's tongue went dry. Straightening her spine, she eyed him over her shoulder. "I didn't know you felt that way."

He met her stare with apparent calm, although the jump of his Adam's apple gave him away. "All my life."

Her jaw dropped.

What?

Everything she thought she knew was wiped from her brain cells and rearranged in an instant. The fishing trip she'd referred to—he'd caught less than Grey because he'd been showing her how to bait the hook. Every fish she'd caught, Toni had unhooked it for her because she didn't want to get her shirt messy.

Two years later, she'd crashed her bike, scraping her knee. The only way to get home had been to sling her arms over the Agrioli boys' shoulders, and hobble while Clay pushed her crippled bike. Once they'd delivered her, Greyson and Clay took off to get the abandoned bikes, while Toni held her hand as her mama dressed her wounds.

Oh, my God.

He'd taken her to homecoming because Grey had injured himself while mending the fence.

Oh. My. God.

Why hadn't she seen it?

———

Antonio

You are such a dick. Christ. He'd kept it in for twenty-four years. Why couldn't he have waited a bit longer? She was still getting over the break-up. And what made him think he even had a shot? Why would she want anything to do with her ex's brother?

Fucking idiot!

Now, they were stuck several yards up on a carnival ride, looking everywhere but at each other. He slid his arm from behind her, removing his jacket and placing it over her shoulders. Embarrassment had him hauling himself into his original seat. Toni didn't know what was worse: facing her or having her body pressed against his side. Either way, he regretted the loss of connection between them.

She crossed her arms, clasping each side of his jacket to pull it closed around her. "I'm sorry; I didn't mean to make things weird. I'm trying to process the bombshell you just dropped."

"I get it. I'm the one that made it awkward."

It took two more goddamn revolutions before they were finally free. "I'll walk you back." Anton grimaced.

"But you still owe me a stuffed toy. And I'm hungry." She attempted to hand him his jacket.

He blinked at the thing. Why did it hurt so much that she wanted to give it back? A return of unwanted goods. Just like she'd rejected his love. "Keep it." *I couldn't take it if I tried.*

Her arm dropped to her side, the jacket hanging limp from her clasped hand. He turned away, forcing his feet not to run, but to walk.

He'd traveled several yards before she caught up, slipping her hand into his, and wearing his jacket. "Thanks for letting me know how you feel."

He laughed without humor. "No problem."

What else was he going to say? *You're welcome. I'm here to stroke your ego anytime, no need to return the favor. At your service. Would you like me to be your doormat too?*

Love like this couldn't be undone. She could walk all over him, and he'd still fucking adore her.

But he wasn't gonna let her do that. Because any kind of relationship was nothing without respect. He'd effectively ruined their friendship. There was no being 'just friends' with someone whom you loved to the depths of your soul. Not after baring your vulnerable truth.

He loosened her grip and pulled out his phone to call Sophia. "Hey. Get dressed. Lory's hungry. You need to make good on your promise."

"What happened?" Sophia questioned.

"Just hurry up. Meet us near the Biscuit Booth." He punched the end button.

"You're leaving?" Lory blinked up at him, hurt darkening her pretty, blue eyes.

"I can't—" Forcing air out through his nostrils, he dropped his gaze to the ground and stowed his cell. "I can't pretend that I don't feel the way I do." He scrubbed a hand over his hair. "Just like you couldn't fake how you felt about Grey."

She winced and turned away.

"You of all people should understand. I'm sorry." Mentioning Grey was a dick move.

And yet, you did it anyway.

"I get it." She gritted out. "Go. You don't need to stay with me. I'll be fine."

Fuuuck. Now he wanted to kick himself. "I'll wait."

"Please don't."

He nodded.
Fair enough.

Chapter EIGHT

Missed the Boat

Antonio

He drove home, pulling the trailer with the cattle behind him, and with a giant stuffed unicorn sitting in the passenger seat. A promise was a promise. It was his final goodbye.

Letting go was the only option.

Why do people play it so fucking cool with each other?

The answer was cowardly, but true.

Because egos are fragile things.

Hiding genuine feelings until the situation was down to the wire, and it was all or nothing, was a program humanity had on repeat. The strength to fess up was often only available when certainty was guaranteed. Either that, or you got to the point where you didn't give a shit about losing anymore, like Anton had. He'd just wanted to crack open his chest and spill out all the pent-up pressure. And if he'd been left spent… so be it.

That was where he was at now. Empty.

In some ironic twist, he felt free. This thing he'd carried around for his entire life—he'd finally unstrapped it. His heart hurt like hell. But he could stretch.

Despite the risk of oncoming pain, if someone sets your soul on fire, they should know.

No matter the outcome.

His mother had told him that when he was a little boy. He hadn't understood it at the time. She'd seemed adamant that he receive the information.

Had she known how he felt about Lory, like his father had?

People were all so fucking afraid that their affection wouldn't be returned, and their hearts would be crushed. Fear was the crippling disease, not love. Doubt and anxiety were an obstruction trapping so many in unfulfilling relationships that were *safe*. Because if they chose someone who didn't push them to the greatest heights, they wouldn't have that far to fall if they were rejected or abandoned.

Real love was intimidating as fuck to a fragile ego.

And that was why people clipped their own wings but still got shitty when they couldn't touch the heavens.

He'd reached for bliss but ruined his chance by pushing too soon.

If he'd had a shot at all.

It was time to let it go now.

Anton pulled into his spot outside the farmhouse. Thankfully, the others hadn't made it back yet. After putting the cattle out to pasture for the night, he headed inside to check on Nonna. Her door was open a crack, and he could see that she was tucked in already. The house was eerily quiet without the usual ruckus from his sisters. Why wouldn't his grandmother use the opportunity to get some rest?

He showered before he found some leftover food in the fridge, scarfing it down in record time. After cleaning his mess, he checked the time; it was eight. Everyone would be home soon. Did he really want to be here when that happened?

Nope.

He sent a text to his mama's phone letting her know he'd be gone for the night, grabbed his keys, then left.

———

Lorelei

Why was it so hard to be honest? To take off her mask and expose her true self to the one person who needed to see her the most—the woman in the mirror. How was it so easy to get caught up in playing the role of good daughter, loyal friend, faithful fiancée, and deny the side of herself that wanted to say, 'Fuck it. I'm gonna do what I want to do, 'cause playing this character is making me miserable?'

She'd been so convincing; *she* hadn't even known her happiness had all been a lie.

Until now.

Lory ran towards the point of light on the horizon she'd seen from her bedroom window. Flames licked the glittering black ink sky. It was him. It had to be. How could he be home sleeping after what had happened? She couldn't fathom going another moment without exposing her heart.

He was so much braver than her. She'd been so caught in grief for her quashed dreams, and guilt and confusion about her growing feelings for Toni, that she'd not been able to see. Love had been there the whole time. He'd helped her uncover the truth in the most abrupt awakening possible.

She'd loved Greyson. She didn't want to discount that. But it had been about playing a role to fulfill expectations—not the least, her own. She'd wanted so much for him to be the one. And all the while Toni had suffered in silence.

That was the killer. The final twist of the blade. The agony of what she'd done to him was as good as turning the knife on herself.

Maybe she was completely insane, running through the fields in the dead of night. Using her phone to illuminate her way, she forced thoughts of coyotes and mountain cats out of her mind and focused solely on getting to him.

At last, she saw his truck. The backdrop of land and trees behind him was a barely discernible silhouette. Antonio sat with his legs hanging over the tray, staring into the campfire. With a blanket over his shoulders, he was as still as the air. His eyes were glazed like he was in a trance. Under a spell. She knew the feeling. For the first time, she understood, and it invigorated her. This was love. She didn't have to chase it or play out some script written by someone else. She could just be.

Dodger came to greet her, escorting her the last few yards to his owner. He sniffed her jeans before curling up beside the truck.

She slowed her steps and came to stand in front of Toni, the fire warming her back. The heat in his eyes scorched her everywhere despite the mixture of sorrow evident in their depths.

"I'm sorry I didn't tell you the truth." She panted on shortened breath. "I've been so confused. And you"—her throat clamped shut and she had to swallow—"you went from zero to a hundred, and I couldn't sort out the guilt from the love. This is…" She huffed. "It's surreal, to be honest."

"What are you saying?" he croaked.

"I'm in love with you, too."

His mouth parted as his chest rose. He threw off the rug and gripped her waist. A second later, she was straddling him, and his mouth was on hers. When Antonio decided to move, he moved, that was for damn sure. The chill of the air bit into her skin as he lifted her shirt to dive his hands underneath. His tongue searched hers, a taste denied for too long. Her arms clamped around his back, holding on. The fire crackled, offering glowing embers to the sky. Her nerve endings lit up, begging for more of his rough touch. He seemed hungry. Like a man who'd starved for too long.

She was the same. She didn't want to think about how fast this was all happening. She just wanted whatever he offered.

His hands palmed her butt and pulled her snug against his erection. He broke the kiss, his breath sawing in and out as he watched her through hooded eyes. It was a question. A request for permission to take this further. She grabbed his face and locked her lips onto his as she ground onto his lap.

Yes. Yes. And yes!

She found herself on her back with Toni's face buried in her cleavage. When had he even unbuttoned her shirt? His hands left her for a second before a blanket descended over them, cocooning them in. Tugging her bra down, he latched onto her nipple, a groan rumbling in his throat. *Oh.* She stretched her neck at the sensation incited by his lapping and sucking. Her hands wandered over the contours of his back. She yanked at his shirt, impatient to get it gone. Rearing up, he ripped it off before lifting her up and undoing her bra strap. Her shirt disappeared next, and he was back on her. Skin on skin. Mouth on mouth. His hips settled between her legs. She lifted the blanket with her feet, pulling it the rest of the way into position before hooking her knees around his waist.

"You're so fucking beautiful. I want you naked in the firelight."

"You're halfway there. Don't stop now," she panted.

He paused for a second, blinking at her. "Fuck." Again, he sat up. Cool air rushed over her skin before he covered her with the rug. "Don't move."

He disappeared over the edge. She heard the truck door open and close before he returned. Lifting the cover at her feet, he dove in from the bottom this time. She waited for him to surface. He didn't. His fingers undid her jeans, dragging them down her legs as he planted kisses on her belly. Wide-eyed, all Lory could do was take in the million stars above, and the flying embers as he bombarded her with a new awareness of her body's capabilities.

His mouth trailed lower. His hands crept higher, covering her breasts. Squeezing. Molding. Making her his. She jerked as he gently bit her sensitive inner thigh. His stubble scratched before his tongue soothed the sting. She cried out as he pinched both nipples and suckled her through the silk of her panties. The sharp edge of teeth on her clit had her clawing at his hair. He dragged in an audible breath as his nose pressed to her mound before placing another kiss there.

She wanted the barrier gone. Just as she was about to beg, he slid them down. She lifted her hips to help. He didn't waste the opportunity to scoop his hands under her butt, parting her with his tongue. Lory gasped.

God. He. Was. Good. *Shit.*

Starting with long, slow licks, he got into a rhythm. Her hips rocked of their own accord. She tossed the blanket away, welcoming the cool air, and the sight of his head between her legs with the fire blazing behind him. Her ankles were bound by the bunched jeans and panties, his torso holding them down. Her knees spread wide to accommodate him. She still had her boots on, like a naughty girl with her pants down. The best kind of mischief.

He slid a finger into her core, scraping his teeth against her bud.

She cried out, trying to keep up with the barrage of sensations. "Antonio."

Two fingers and hard sucking had her spine curling. He spread her open with his thumb and forefinger, his elbow pressing into her thigh. Inside, his fingers stroked while his tongue swirled and sucked. Stubble scratched in a delicious added bonus.

She came like a freight train. And yes, she was a screamer.

He growled, the vibrations from his mouth adding to the onslaught. He stayed with her as she rode the wave, somehow knowing when to ease off, but not abandoning her in mid climax. She swore it went on for minutes.

Her breathing slowed. She heard the hiss of a zip and the rip of a packet. He tugged off her boots and clothes before grasping her feet in each hand. Folding her legs back, he surged forward, positioning himself at her entrance. She curled her palms around the backs of her thighs, straining to see the features of his silhouetted face.

"Are you okay?" His question probed her mind, the forerunner for what was to come.

She nodded, not trusting her voice to work.

He rubbed the underside of his cock along her folds, massaging the sensitive bundle of nerves at the crest. They both exhaled in sync. Thrusting, he entered to the hilt.

For a long moment neither of them moved. A riot of emotions she hadn't been prepared for pummeled her heart, brain, and body.

An overture to belonging and destiny.

An undeniable promise of the fulfilment of dreams.

A homecoming.

He placed her feet on his shoulders before dragging his palms along the backs of her thighs to rest on top of her hands. Her legs went to jelly as he stroked deeply. Sweat-slicked skin slapped against each other as they gasped for oxygen. She shifted her legs to circle his hips, hooking her ankles behind him. His hands wedged under her back to lift her into his lap. He guided her arms around his neck before sliding his grip to her ass. Kisses feathered over her face. His hips pumped into hers. "Even better"—he gasped—"than I imagined."

Electricity coursed along her nerves, setting off detonations wherever it went. She quaked as pleasure again seized her body. His hands bit into her skin as he ground their centers together. He locked his silver stare onto hers, a world of emotion caught in one look before finally grunting his release.

Lory rested her head on his shoulder, trying to calm her system. Her body went lax. "Are you okay, sweetheart?" He held her against him while he switched positions so she lay on top. The blanket made a reappearance as their temperatures returned to equilibrium.

She nodded into his neck, kissing the spot where she nuzzled. *Better than okay.* Teetering on the edge of bliss and exhaustion, it was impossible to voice her answer. She hoped he understood that he'd set something free in her. A part of herself she hadn't realized had been imprisoned. His fingers drew patterns on her back. Love notes written in calligraphy. An exposition she'd cherish for eternity. Their heart beats drummed against each other, finally finding the perfect rhythm. They stayed there until the fire died and the sun's rays bled into morning.

Chapter NINE

Magnolia Tree

Antonio

He took her home, leaving the truck in the south paddock and walking her the rest of the way. She snuck in the house before texting him a minute later.

Got to my room just before Daddy went downstairs. Great timing.

He scrubbed a hand over his face as he returned to his truck. *Jesus.* That had been close. He'd have to be more careful in future. But it had been too damn hard to let her go.

When can I see you again? He typed the words and then hit the delete button, erasing his eagerness.

Be cool.

Glad you're safe.

He'd scared her away once. He didn't want to do it again. They needed to slow down. Yeah, he'd been in love with her for more than twenty years. But this was new for her. He wanted to give her all the time she needed to see him as *hers*.

He pulled the truck in front of the farmhouse before making his way straight to the shower.

"Where have you been?" Papà's voice pulled him up short just shy of his destination.

Shit. Anton didn't turn around, reaching for the door handle. The only face he wanted in his mind right now was Lory's. Especially her firelit expression when she'd watched him go down on her. Parted lips, hooded eyes, pupils that almost engulfed the blue of her irises. Damn, he was getting hard again.

"I camped out in the field." He cracked open the bathroom door, smelling his mother's herbal shampoo.

"Did you put out the fire properly?"

"*Sì*, Papà." Ducking into the room, he kicked the door closed behind him.

He turned on the shower a bit colder than usual and ran through a list of all the jobs he had to do.

Get the hay feeders ready.

Do a lice check and treatment.

Check the rye grass for blast…

Lory.

Lory.

Lory.

Water cascaded over his head as he stared at the drain. He'd managed to distract himself from thoughts of her for years by keeping busy. That trick wasn't working now.

And his cock was still hard.

Wrapping a palm around his length, he squeezed the head gently before sliding up and down. Remembering the feel of her pressed against him, his cock buried deep inside her, it took less than a minute for him to come.

He soaped up, rinsed off and towel-dried before hearing a knock at the door. Covering up, he opened it a crack.

Sophia and Marianne.

He groaned. *Jesus, not now.* "What?"

Marianne, being taller, stood behind Sophia. Both of their faces lined up within the narrow gap he'd allowed for the exchange.

"We're just checking to see if you're okay?" Sophia assumed the position of spokesperson, as per usual.

"I'm fine."

"You didn't seem fine when you left." Marianne mumbled.

"And neither did Lory," Sophia added with more volume.

He sighed, knowing from experience that they wouldn't back off. It was better not to be cornered in a room with only one exit, which they had blocked. Making sure the towel was secure, he yanked the door open and charged past his sisters.

"You need to make things right." Sophia was like Dodger gnawing at a bone.

Oh, I did. "What makes you think things are wrong?" he threw over his shoulder as he headed for his room.

"I was the one you called to come and clean up your mess after you ditched her, remember?"

"I didn't ditch her." Annoyance sharpened his voice. He and Lory were so far past the hurt and misunderstanding of that night. Not that Sophia had any clue. And it was none of his sisters' goddamn business, as far as he was concerned.

He spun around, slapping his palms on the doorframe to bar their entry. Sophia pulled up short, Marianne, bumping into her back.

"Sure looked like ya did." Sophia raised one dark brow.

"I know you mean well, but I've got it covered. Okay?"

Marianne grasped her sister by the shoulders, tugging her back. Sophia folded her arms and stood her ground.

He narrowed his eyes. "Time for you to leave. Unless you want to see me in my birthday suit?"

Marianne lifted her hands and backed away, disgust screwing her nose up. Sophia huffed and met his stare.

He loosened the towel but didn't let it fall.

She squeaked, turning to march away.

Laughing, he closed the door and got dressed.

Maybe Sophia had a point. Maybe he did need to make sure she was okay. He and Lory hadn't exactly done much talking after she'd confessed her feelings. He'd basically pounced on her. *Shit.* He should check on her tonight.

Any excuse to see her again.

Anton parked in the paddock bordering on the Carters' land and jumped the fence. Their house sat in the next field to the south. The full moon lit the way as he walked across the pasture. A group of cows huddled together under a tree. A series of moos let him know they were watching.

He reached the house to find that her light was already out. *Shit.* It *was* late. But he didn't want to chicken out now. Thanking whoever had decided to plant a Southern Magnolia near the house, Anton climbed its branches. He hopped on the roof of the veranda before creeping over to Lory's room. Straightening his shirt, he gave himself a mental pat on the back. *All without disturbing the peace.*

He pulled out his phone and typed a message. **Hey. Are you awake?**

A dim light broached the edge of the curtains. **Yeah. Can't sleep.**

He frowned. **Why not?**

I can't stop thinking about last night.

His face split into a grin. **Need me to help you get some shut-eye?**

I wish.

His chest expanded as love rampaged inside. God, he needed to hold her. **Open your window.**

Why???

Because I don't want to break it to get to you.

The curtain was shoved to the side and Lory's silhouette appeared. She opened the glass. "How did you get up here?"

"I climbed the tree. Let me in," he whispered.

"You're crazy."

"Aw, come on. Don't tell me you've never made use of that tree before."

"When I was young and dumb, maybe."

Lory winked, a wicked glint in her make-up free baby blues, hair wild around her face. How could one simple twitch of an eyelid mock such innocence? She was wearing pink pajamas covered in cartoon cherries, for Christ's sake. She was fucking adorable.

And completely edible.

Whoa, back up.

Anton clambered into the room, crossing to sit on the edge of her bed. "Come here." Holding his arms wide, he beckoned her over.

She melted into his embrace, sinking her back into his chest, and resting her head on his shoulder. "I'm so glad you're here."

Hope squeezed his heart while doubt spiked his thoughts. "Are you?"

She sat forward, twisting to look at him with hurt in her eyes. "Yes."

Disbelief had been a reflex. A habit after years of denial. "Sorry. I've been dreaming of this for so long, I guess it's hard to believe it's real."

She stood before crawling into bed and tucking herself under the covers. Giving him a small smile, she patted the space beside her. "Tell me something?"

"Sure." He took off his shoes and jacket, choosing to lie on top of the sheets.

"When did you know you loved me?" Her sleepy eyes blinked at him.

He rolled to face her; one side of his mouth quirked. "I had a crush on you when we were both still in diapers. But I knew it was love when you were the first person I wanted to share things with. Anytime I had a win or a problem, it was you I had to tell. You encouraged me. You have a way of making me see the other side of things… and then you got boobs."

She smacked him in the chest. He grinned, kissing her forehead.

"I have a confession." Her finger traced the line of his jaw.

"Okay?"

"I think I've secretly had a thing for you for years."

What? His eyes darted to hers as blood surged through his veins.

Triumph and tragedy warred for supremacy. So much time wasted. He wanted to roar at the injustice. Had that collar of unrequited love been a delusion the whole time? If it had, he could finally breathe.

"You were always so thoughtful and sweet. I started to look forward to seeing you just as much as Grey, if not more. I had to pull away. It wasn't even a conscious thing. It was self-protection. I was loyal to him. I couldn't love you too." She pressed a palm against her forehead. "I feel like I've betrayed Grey by admitting it, but it's true. I've been so confused. I loved him. I really did. But I knew something was missing. He never wanted to… be physically intimate." Her hand lowered to her throat, fingers blanching the skin as she pressed and took a pause.

Anton stayed silent, her tumble of words clicking into place one by one as they constructed the truth. Slowly, his eyebrows migrated so far north they almost frosted over.

She'd seemed to be in love. And they'd never…?

Never?

"And his kisses were friendly at best. I thought maybe he wanted to save that part for marriage. But he never really included me in his long-term plans. It's obvious now that I was under some illusion. I think he asked me to marry him because everybody expected it. And he was willing to settle with me. At the time, anyway. But he couldn't pretend to be happy on the farm as much as I could never have continued pretending to be happy in a passionless relationship." She dropped her finger and rolled to her back. "I cheated on him."

Holy. Fucking. Shit.

Anton's lungs took a few seconds' pause, barring any movement of air.

He could judge her for her actions. Label her deceitful and every other word used for people who cross the boundaries of their relationships. But he didn't blame her. The torment was clear in the tremble of her voice and the tears spilling into her hair. She thought she was a horrible person because she'd cheated. On whom? A fake boyfriend? *Goddamn you, Grey.*

Christ. Some people were excellent at hiding their pain. The façade they showed society was watertight, airtight, nuclear-blast-proof, you name it. The only way to destroy it was from the inside out. A self-imposed implosion.

Pretense was a damn heavy thing.

"The week of the rodeo two years back, he disappeared for a couple of nights. I knew he was with another woman. I saw him leave with her. So, I found myself a cowboy from out of town. He invited me into his trailer. I got drunk and gave away my virginity." Both hands came up to cover her face. "You're the only person I've told. I don't want there to be any secrets between us. Do you think badly of me now?"

That fucking asshole. Both the cowboy and his brother. His nostrils flared.

Anton pulled her shield away, needing her to see the sincerity in his eyes. "No. I think you've been hurting for a long time. And I'm sorry my brother is such a son of a bitch."

"He wanted to do right by me. Everybody wanted to see us together, but we were never meant to be."

Hell no, they weren't. He'd known that for years.

Decades.

Anton sat up, leaning against the headboard. He hadn't realized how much resentment he'd harbored for his brother. It pulsed in his temples and gripped him by the neck, a force holding him in place and boiling his blood.

He almost shook with the effort it took to calm himself down. It wasn't doing him any good holding on to the hurt. He knew Grey thought he'd been doing the right thing. He hadn't seen that Lory was sincere in her affections. Anton understood that Grey had a sense of responsibility towards Lory. He'd sworn to look after her when they were young, and he'd stuck to his promise. Until he was miserable. He'd twisted his life into a picture of what Papà and Mama wanted for him. The heir to the empire, set to marry the girl next door. The Carters and Agriolis joined in a merger of beef titans. Greyson hadn't wanted any of it. He and Lory had both been trapped in an abstract version of somebody else's family portrait.

It was time to paint a new picture. The realist version.

"Sweetheart, Grey can't see past his own nose most of the time. You're right about him wanting to fulfill expectations. He made himself sick with it. Until he got angry. Not at you. At himself for falling into the trap and dragging you with him. It's time to let it go. We've got each other now."

"I'm so sorry for the pain I've caused you." Her tears flowed in rivers now.

Anton jumped off the bed, yanking back the covers. He climbed in beside her and tucked her against his body.

"You've made me the happiest cowboy in Mississippi." He pressed a kiss to her forehead. "Ain't no need to apologize for that."

Chapter TEN

Cherry Pie With Cream

Lorelei

November

Lorelei stashed the picnic basket behind the shed, shooing Dodger away as he came to investigate. Sniffing around the wicker, he let out little yips and growls.

"Shh. You're gonna give me away," she whispered. He buried his snout in her hand before tossing his nose up, as if to say, 'Pat me.' She could never resist his advances and buried her fingers in his fur. The dog had her heart, well and truly.

Like all the Agriolis,

She could hear Antonio whistling behind the wall. Since their first night together, they'd hadn't managed much more than a few stolen kisses in the spot where she stood now. The want had begun to gnaw at her insides.

She peeked around the corner. Antonio's back was turned as he grabbed something from the shelf. Lory snuck up behind him and covered his eyes. He tensed, his hands grasping her forearms to pull them away before spinning to face her.

"Hi." Her grin morphed into shock when she caught his look of hunger. "How are y—" He didn't waste a second before locking lips with hers. She opened to him, letting the rush of passion take over. Thank God they were on the same page.

Her body was the match and he was the friction.

She'd never been kissed the way Toni kissed her. The touch of his lips infused her with some drug that wiped her brain cells. His arms clamped around her back before he lifted her. She wrapped her legs around his waist. He responded by adjusting his hold, grabbing her ass.

She broke off the kiss, gasping for air. "Do you think your family will miss you if you don't show up for lunch?"

His mouth landed on her collarbone, his tongue flicking out for a taste. "Don't care." Two big palms gripped her ass tighter as he pulled her center in to line up with his arousal. "What'd you have in mind?"

Heat bloomed in her core. She fought for breath. *This man... oh, lordy be.* Closing her eyes, she tried to collect her scattered thoughts. "Uh. A... a picnic." She gasped as he worked her through her jeans. "By the r-river."

His head snapped up. "Let's go."

With a swift move, he had her on the four-wheeler.

"Wait! I've got to grab the basket." She slipped down and ran to collect their food. Dodger bounced on his front legs, apparently wanting in on the excitement.

She returned, passing the pack to Toni so he could secure it in the rack bag while she took her seat. After washing his hands, he jumped on in front.

He reached behind to place his palms on her knees, then glided them up her thighs. "I love having your legs wrapped around me."

Her gut clenched, her body ready and willing to be stripped naked and laid out on the soft grass for him. *Damn.* He knew just what to say to seduce her. She gripped him around the waist, wanting to find somewhere private ASAP.

The engine rumbled to life.

The dog jumped in his lap.

"Not today, buddy." Anton put the ball of fur on the ground, and Dodger skulked away with his tail between his legs.

She leaned around Toni's shoulder. "Aw. You didn't have to do that."

He peered back through hooded eyes. "I want you all to myself."

Holy shit.

Sorry, Dodger. "Let's go."

The thrum of the engine and his ass rubbing against her inner thighs did wonders for her libido. As if it wasn't stoked on high already.

Within five minutes, they'd arrived at a clearing beside the stream where the grassy bank sloped down to greet the river. Cypress and willow trees brushed the water's edge a few yards farther along. They'd had a week without rain, so the flow was gentle and inviting. Although she hadn't prepared for a swim, she had bared her arms to the sun's subtle November warmth.

He got off first before plucking her from the seat. "You got a picnic blanket in here?"

"Yup." She nodded as he pulled the basket from the rack.

After placing their supplies down, he walked to the water's edge and ran his hands under the water. "You ever skinny dipped?"

She paused to steady herself as the thought of being naked and naughty with him sent adrenaline coursing through her veins. "Never. Have you?"

"When I was five," he laughed.

"Is the water cold?" She folded her arms above her head, tilting her face to the sun.

"Chilly as a schoolmarm."

Her limbs dropped as she gaped at him. "A schoolmarm?"

"Haven't you ever heard Mama say that?"

She followed his lead, rinsing the dirt from her skin. Goosepimples sprang to attention as the freezing liquid flowed between her fingers. "No. She must've had *some* teacher when she was a kid."

He shrugged. "She never talks about it."

Lory helped him spread out the rug before setting the food on their plates.

Pouring the lemonade, Toni assessed the spread. "Potato salad. Coleslaw. Buffalo wings… you've been busy."

"I was hungry." Starving for him. And yeah, food.

"What's for dessert?"

Me.

Me, me, me. "Cherry pie with cream."

Air rushed from his nostrils. "You're killin' me."

She raised a brow. "You look alive."

"Can we have dessert first?" His fingers tiptoed up her leg.

I know exactly what kind of sweetness you're after, buddy. Yes, please, and thank you. "No. Be a gentleman." *Or don't.* She giggled and sent him a wink.

He bit his knuckle, groaning before picking up a plate. "You're a tease."

Yes. And you love it.

Lory laughed as she took her serving. Damn, if he didn't have her in a playful mood. She decided to toy with him some more. Lifting a wing to her mouth, she kept her eyes on Toni as she took a bite. His eyelids peeled wide. Sucking on the bone, she slowly devoured the meat, making love to it until she finally licked her fingers clean. His food lay abandoned on his plate, his attention fixed on her antics.

"Aren't you hungry?" She pursed her lips to hide a smirk.

"Ravenous." His gaze roamed her body.

Setting the grin free, Lory speared a piece of potato with her fork. "Eat."

He polished off his food in a flash, setting his dish aside before diving for her. "Let me help you with that." Stealing the fork from her grip, he put it on her plate before bringing it to his lap. "I wanna feed you. I love watching you eat."

She swallowed, almost choking on her own saliva.

"What'll you have next?" He lifted the selection for her perusal.

Eyebrows raised, she blurted, "More potato, please."

It should have been weird. Or maybe made her feel like a child. But it had the opposite effect. With each mouthful, he cherished her, staring intently as she chewed and swallowed. A wave of heat chased the path of his focus across her skin. She reached mindlessly to unbutton her shirt. It couldn't have been much more than seventy degrees out, but damn, it was hot.

"What are you doing?" His husky drawl betrayed his arousal.

"It's time for some sugar."

"That's exactly what I was thinking." He ditched the leftovers and finished freeing the remaining buttons. "Let me take care of you."

Lorelei whimpered. *Oh my God.*

Fabric was peeled from her skin, her inhibitions dropping with it. His touch held a reverence that reached beyond the flesh, obliterating any lingering doubts or fears of surrendering her heart to him.

She was all his.

And the fire in his stare said he knew it.

Reaching behind his neck, he yanked the T-shirt from his back, baring the next course to her hungry eyes. Lory's mouth watered. *Dayum. Ain't nothin' as fine as an Italian cowboy.* The man was an ad for

Wrangler and a hard day's work. Dark hair, eyes like steel, a torso rendered with endless contours and angles for her to trace.

With my tongue.

Antonio straddled her legs, reaching into the basket to retrieve the whipped cream and cherry pie. Licking his lips, he homed in on her naked breasts. "I promise I'll clean any mess I make."

Her breath stopped as she collapsed on the rug. *Holy Mary, mother of...*

He hovered over her, painting his desire with cherry filling from her nipples to her navel. Running his sticky fingers over her mouth, he urged her to open for a taste. She sucked him in, reveling in his hooded stare and the feel of his bulge under her wandering hand. Her tongue laved the sugariness until his flavor took over.

She wanted more. Gripping his wrist, she tugged until his digits popped free. Her pulse hammered as she guided him to her soaked panties, the final hindrance to her nakedness. At first, he pressed gently, chewing on his cheek. Concentration pulled his brows together. Lory resisted the urge to beg as suspense fueled her excitement. She lifted herself onto her elbows to see what his next move would be.

Toni hooked the top of the satin and dragged her underwear off. She was as bare as she'd been the day she was born. Exposed to the sun, the cool breeze, and his hot-blooded intentions. Sliding his touch between her legs, he trailed a path to her center, eyes fixed on her shuddering chest when he reached his destination.

His gaze locked with hers. "It's a sin to have pie without cream." Pushing two fingers inside, he mimicked what he'd done to her mouth.

Lory gasped before releasing a moan, stretching her arms over her head. Her spine bowed as she looked to the heavens to give thanks. The cold shock of whipped cream dropping onto her skin had her head snapping up. One nipple. Two nipples. Around her navel. On the juncture of her thighs. He prepped her to be devoured. Her breath came in shallow pants as he braced his palms either side of her and bowed his head. Using his lips and tongue, he loved one side before kissing and licking across to the other. He wasn't joking about cleaning up after himself. As he moved lower, she got up on her elbows again, not wanting to miss a second of the action.

Somewhere along the way, he'd undone the top button of his jeans and the tip of his cock peeked out.

"Do I get to have dessert too?"

"Mm." He worked his tongue around her belly button.

Was that a reply or an expression of how much he liked her pie?

"Toni."

"Mm?"

"Get rid of your pants."

"Later." He dragged his tongue up her center, sampling the sweetness.

She moaned, wanting to do the same to him. "I wanna lick you while you taste me."

He froze, immobile for so long. *Oh, shit.* She held her breath. Had she said something wrong? She'd never done this before. Her fingers twitched with the urge to gather her clothes and rebuild the defense he'd so lovingly peeled away.

Toni finally moved, resting his forehead on her belly. "You're perfect."

She sat up, lifting his head so she could kiss him. A wordless declaration that she'd never wanted anything or anyone more than she wanted him. *You're perfect, too.* Being out in the open only made their coming together more incredible. More daring. She wanted to explore so many possibilities with him. Her heart thumped, waiting for a sign.

He gripped the denim, shoving his jeans down. Her lungs inflated before a sharp exhale.

He wants this.

He took a seat on the rug, wrestling his pants off all the way while she reached for the cream. He was hard and ready, the veins on his silky skin standing out. His length bobbed as she added the topping. Running her tongue over the tip, she collected a sample. *Yum.* Toni grunted in response. She turned, finding him watching her through heavy lids. Her heart stuttered. The man was a smorgasbord all for her.

She threw a leg over his waist and faced his feet. His palms curled over her hips, tugging her backwards. She shuffled as he tucked his arms under her, spreading her with his shoulders. He pulled her down. Hot, moist flesh struck hot, moist flesh, the impact expelling a cry and bending her spine.

She wanted her mouth on him. Gripping him at the base, she lapped all the dessert. Her pelvis rolled into his touch. He took from her as she took from him.

Their bodies joined in an endless loop of flesh and skin. Infinite love in motion. Tongues explored. Palms squeezed. She bobbed her head, sucking and licking.

Cool air skimmed her core as his head flopped on the rug. "Fuck. I can't hold on."

His curse kicked off an adrenaline rush, feeding her determination to give him pleasure. Adding her hands, she worked him harder. His fingers dug into her. Flattening the soles of his feet on the ground, his hips jerked in short, sharp bursts until he finally let go. Heated breath rushed over her center as he cursed again. There was no chance to revel in her victory. His tongue drove into her, setting her off-balance. Slapping her palms on his hipbones, she reared up. His strong grip held her tightly in place, letting her know he was in control now. And she let him take what he wanted.

Sweet surrender.

The sunlight reflected off their slick skin. The breeze teased her hair as his mouth laved her folds. He eased his hold and she rocked into his movements, the pressure building. Overcome with complete abandon, she rode him unabashedly. Bared to him. Bared to nature. Stars danced behind her lids as her eyes rolled back. Pleasure burst from her core, shattering her to pieces.

Still in a haze of ecstasy, Lory barely knew where she was before he'd scooted out from beneath her.

Tipping her forward onto her elbows, he sank to the hilt into her pulsing heat. "So fucking good. I love being inside you."

She couldn't stop her cries of pleasure. Waves of ecstasy pulled her into some other realm. A low rumble vibrated from his chest as he slammed her from behind. He palmed one breast; his other hand fisted into the rug near her arm. His thrusts became erratic, his shaft throbbing inside her. He dropped his face between her shoulder blades, finally breaking apart.

Lory collapsed on the blanket, exhausted from the workout but completely satiated.

And mindlessly in love.

He kissed along her spine, then pulled away before helping her up.

She spun in his arms and planted a kiss on his lips. "That was amazing."

He grinned. "You're amazing. I love you."

Pulling her closer, he plied her face with kisses. Across her cheeks and her nose. Over her forehead. She giggled, swatting him away.

Then he froze before she heard an audible swallow. After loosening the embrace, he gripped her by the arms. "Oh, fuck." His face turned pale as he stared down at her in horror.

"What? What's wrong?"

"We didn't use a condom."

"It's okay, I'm on the pill." Heat flushed her face in a ridiculous show of chagrin. Particularly after what they'd just done. Turning away, she searched for her underwear.

"Oh. Good." He smiled. "How about that skinny dip?" He snatched the panties she'd just retrieved, holding them up like a flag. His grin wide enough to show off most of his teeth.

"Hey!" She jumped, reaching for the satin. He was too damn tall.

They'd played this game once before. He'd pinched a Judy Blume novel from her when she was thirteen.

And I got it back before he'd finished one sentence. Lory smiled as she dug her fingers into his ribs.

He flinched, dropping the underwear on the rug.

Ha! Gotcha... oh, shit!

Catching her in a bear hug, he lifted her off her feet before she could grab them. "I promised to clean up any mess. I don't think I did a good enough job."

That was true. Their skin was sticky from the dessert, among *other things*. Distracted by the press of their bodies, she wasn't prepared for the shock of cold water. A scream ripped from her throat as a belly laugh tumbled from his mouth.

"Fuck, it's cold," she spluttered.

"Screamer."

She opened her mouth to serve him a retort, but his kiss cut her off.

Her limbs wrapped around his warmth.

And before long, they had steam curling off their bodies.

Chapter
ELEVEN

Nighttime Visits

Lorelei

December

A thump outside her window startled her awake. *Shit. I fell asleep.* She bolted upright, her novel tumbling off her chest to the floor, and rubbed her eyes. A tap sounded on the glass. Stumbling over, she lifted the dormer for him to climb through.

"Shh," she hissed, immediately wondering why she'd bothered. *So what if we get caught?*

TV noise drifted upstairs. Squealing tires and gunshots. Chances were, nobody would hear them anyways.

"Sorry. I texted but you didn't answer." He stretched to his full height before pulling her into a hug. "Did I wake you?"

Burying her face in his chest, she pulled in his scent with a deep breath. Soap and man. "I didn't mean to doze off. I felt a little out of sorts, so I came to bed early. I wanted to wait for you."

"It's okay. You're tired. Do you want me to leave?"

No. She shook her head, gripping him tighter. Two months, they'd been together. Weeks of furtive glances and illicit liaisons. Moments as slippery as black ice. She was very much in danger of falling and breaking her heart. Why did he still want to hide their relationship?

"Lie down. I wanna hold you." His whisper teased her ear.

Lory crawled into bed, rubbing her unsettled tummy while he took off his boots and coat. "I've missed you."

"Same."

Then why are we still sneaking around? "When are we going to tell everyone?"

Nobody had said a word, but their families weren't stupid. Her parents had eyeballed her with suspicion a few times after she'd disappeared for a 'walk.' Was Toni ashamed of being with her because she'd been with his brother? Like she was secondhand goods?

Lory breathed through her nose, trying to calm her system. She wanted to go out. On an actual date. In public. But they were still stealing moments in the fields, and he was still climbing the magnolia tree.

His brows dipped. "I'm not ready for anyone else's opinion."

Her throat cramped. Yep, he was embarrassed. "Are you worried they'll be disappointed?"

His head jerked back as a groove carved into his forehead. He joined her on the mattress, propped on his side to face her. "Hell, no. It's none of anybody else's business. Is that what you think? They don't want to see us together?"

She bit her lip, reluctant to express her fears. But hiding things like that would only make them fester and grow out of proportion. "I'm worried *you* don't want them to see us together."

His mouth parted on a huff as he stared at her. "I've been a dick." Pinching the bridge of his nose, he groaned softly.

"No, that's not what I meant."

He dropped his hand to reveal eyes filled with remorse. "I have. I was selfish, not wanting to share you, and I made you think I was hiding you like a dirty secret."

Okay, yeah. You did.

"For the record, my family know how I feel about you. They knew before I told you. Apparently, my poker face sucks."

Oh. The knot in her stomach loosened. That explained why Sophia had foisted her onto Toni at the fair. Bless her cotton socks. Lory owed his sister big time. "Why don't you use the front door next time you come over?"

He slid an arm under her breasts, tucking his chin in her shoulder. "Are you ready to tell your family?"

"Yes. I want to spend Christmas with you. Thanksgiving was miserable."

"I bought you a present the other day." He pressed kisses along her throat.

She tilted her head to give him more room. *God, it's nearly Christmas.* "Did you? I only have one more gift to buy then I'm done."

Toni pulled back to meet her gaze. "Is it mine?"

She shook her head. "Nope. I got yours ages ago."

His eyes flashed; the grey almost eclipsed by the black of his pupils in the dim light. "What is it?"

She elbowed him in the side. "Be patient."

"It's only a week away. I can hack it."

She stiffened. "What?"

"I can wait."

"Did you say it's next week?" Her brain churned with numbers, adding them together, taking them away. None of it seemed to make sense. *How was Christmas a week away?*

He sat up, eyeing her with concern. "Yeah. You okay?"

Ah, I don't know. "Mm-hmm."

He combed her hair back from her face before placing a kiss on her temple. "You're tired. I'm gonna go. I'll call you tomorrow."

"Okay." Her hands gripped the covers. She was tempted to yank them over her head.

"Night, sweetheart." Toni pecked her on the lips and put his jacket and shoes on before crawling out the way he'd come.

She stared at the ceiling, her stomach doing flips.

Christmas was the twenty-fifth, which meant it was about the eighteenth today.

How had she lost track of the time?

What the hell was the date?

What the hell did it matter?

They'd been dating for a couple of months at least. Two months, during which she hadn't had a period.

Oh. Fuck.

Chapter
TWELVE

Here's the Thing...

Lorelei

Christmas Eve

"Mama!" Lory yelled up the stairs.

"Yes?" Her mom appeared on the landing at the top.

"I'm just going to the store."

Her stomach hadn't allowed her to do a whole hell of a lot over the last week. She'd put Toni off, telling him she didn't want to make him sick. Maybe there was no avoiding that outcome? God, how was he going to take the news?

Today was the last opportunity to finish her preparations before Christmas. And for what she needed to buy, she had to leave town.

Her mama's eyes searched her features. "Oh, are you sure you're well enough?"

"I'm fine, Mama." She yanked the corners of her mouth upwards, aiming for sincerity.

Her mother raised a brow, clearly not buying the act. "Can you grab some things while you're out, please? The list is on the kitchen table."

"Okay." She turned away quickly.

"Thanks, baby girl."

Baby girl.

Yeah, not so much.

How would Mama react when she found out her baby might be pregnant?

Lory stowed some crackers in her pocketbook before checking her wallet for cash. If she was going to buy a pregnancy test, she'd have to drive to the next county. Wagging tongues were the worst part of small country towns. Taking a drink bottle with her, she took off, still deciding on a destination.

Driving south, she cut through the De Soto National Forest, headed for the Walmart in Wiggins. The shadows of the trees beat against her car, delivering a public flogging. *Sinner, sinner, chicken dinner.* For all the progress society had made, it was still frowned upon to have a baby out of wedlock. Lord help her if she saw anybody she knew. She was banking on the fact that most townsfolk went to Hattiesburg on account of it being closer.

Exiting the car, she nibbled on a cracker, and sipped water before going in. There wasn't a question in her mind of whether she was pregnant or not. Her 'tummy bug' hadn't eased. She was getting damn good at hiding out at dinner time. Nothing smelled right anymore. Least of all her mama's cooking.

Lory made her way to the pharmacy and purchased the test, before finding a restroom. That was the other thing—she needed to pee all the damn time. A few minutes later she was in the cubicle, staring at two blue lines.

And there it was. The end of life as she knew it.

How was she going to tell Toni? Christmas was tomorrow. Maybe she could tell him they were both on Santa's naughty list? And instead of a lump of coal, he'd given them a baby.

It would probably be the end of another relationship.

Wasn't she just kickin' goals and takin' names?

Antonio

Antonio unloaded sacks of supplemental feed from his truck, stacking them in the barn. He'd been lifting shit all damn day. His back muscles ached. His legs burned from climbing in and out of the tray. This was a job Grey and he used to share. One would build the pile while the other emptied the truck, passing the goods between them. Doing it all himself was something else. He wiped the sweat off his brow with his sleeve before reaching for his water bottle.

He needed to quit whining. Even if it was in his head. Truth was, he was pissed. He hadn't seen Lory in a week. He didn't doubt she was sick, but his gut told him something else was going on. Was she having second thoughts? Maybe she did still love Grey after all. Seven days of sparse communication had all his fears clawing to the surface trying to pull him under.

The sound of approaching footsteps had his head turning.

"Hey." Lory leaned on the frame of the barn door, her face sallow and sunken, but still infinitely beautiful.

Ask and ye shall receive.

"I've been trying to phone you." *Nice greeting, Anton.*

Her nose wrinkled before she dropped her chin.

He was a jackass. She seemed to curl in on herself, clothes hanging loose on her slight frame. "Sorry. Are you still sick?"

"Not exactly." She bit her lips.

What does that mean? He moved to stand in front of her. "Why didn't you answer my calls?"

She shook her head more times than was necessary. "I couldn't talk. But I'm okay."

"You don't look okay." *Christ! Shut the fuck up with the compliments.*

"Thanks?" She glared at him.

"No. That's not"—He squeezed the bridge of his nose—"I can see the shadows under your eyes. You haven't even responded to my messages."

Tears welled in her eyes as she thrust out her hand. Inside it, she held a white plastic stick. He squinted, trying to make sense of what it was.

Is that? No. What?

"Are you pregnant?" His brows headed for the wild blue yonder.

She sniffed, nodding as tears rolled down her cheeks.

Fuck. He took a step backwards, fingers diving into his hair as if doing that could hold him upright while his insides collapsed to the straw-covered dirt.

Hooooly shit.

He pulled his palms down to grip the back of his neck and visualized their plans vaporizing to dust.

She wanted to study. They both did. How were they going to do that now?

They'd need their own home.

Papà would be furious.

Would he kick me out?

What if I lose my job?

How was he going to support them?

How were they going to raise a child?

His heart galloped out of control as the rest of him turned to ice. A cold sweat broke out across his skin. The two useless sacs of air in his ribcage refused to work.

So much for using condoms. . .

But she was on the pill. . .

He stood there for God knew how long attempting to reconcile the fact that he was going to be a father. His mind whirred to a halt as a tiny piece of joy sparked to life.

Holy shit. I'm going to be a papà!

All those plans were still within reach, the timeline just needed a bit of rearranging. Anton had no idea how much time had passes while he frantically reorganized their lives in his head. When he was finally back in the land of the living, Lory had disappeared, and the sun had moved an awful long way across the sky.

Oh, Jesus. He'd scared her away. *No.*

He pulled out his phone, bringing up her number.

"Hey, this is Lory! You know what to do…"

Beep.

Message bank. Damn it.

"Lory. Where are you? We need to talk about this."

His hands shook as adrenaline assaulted his system. He needed to calm the fuck down or he wouldn't even be able to walk, let alone drive.

He hit redial.

No answer.

The call cut off as his phone buzzed with an incoming call from Clay.

"Clay."

"Do you know what's goin' on with Lory? She took off to the airport."

"The airport?"

"Yeah. Boston. Is Grey up to more bullshit? Because I swear, I will have his balls if he so much as touches a hair on her head."

Anton clenched the phone a little tighter as he ground his teeth. She'd gone running back to Grey. With Anton's baby in her belly.

His arm dropped to his side as an avalanche of emotions gathered momentum.

Damn if that wasn't a sword straight through the heart.

Chapter THIRTEEN

Boston

Lorelei

Lory dragged her feet to the exit of Boston Logan, the crowd around her making her feel like a snail. Everybody in such a rush, probably desperate to get home for Christmas. And here she was, desperate to get away.

The sliding doors opened, letting in a gust of frigid North Atlantic air. She halted her steps. "Jesus H. Christ, it's freezing!"

"Move." A woman barged past, tossing a curse over her shoulder as a farewell.

Bless your heart, honey. "Sorry." Standing off to the side, Lory fished in her pockets for her gloves. "I'd better not get frostbite." She grabbed the lapels of her coat and pulled them together before breaching the doorway.

The queue to get a cab stretched for yards. Taking out the water bottle the flight attendant had given her, she tentatively sipped its contents. Her hand felt around for the cheese and crackers she'd stashed but didn't retrieve the prize. The way her stomach was twisting, she wasn't game to try anything solid anyways.

This was the worst idea ever. *Why am I here?*

The answer hit her like a sour grape.

She'd always done this.

Any time she'd been in trouble or needed soothing, she went straight to Greyson. He'd been her best friend, her protector. He would lead; she'd follow. He was safe. Easy. He treated her like something precious to be kept in a display case. Y'all can look, but you can't touch.

Toni didn't do that. He encouraged her to try new experiences and expand her horizons. He put her on edge in a good way. She flicked through her catalogue of time with the Agrioli men, a realization derailing her train of thought.

Had she always run to Greyson?

He would probably disagree. In truth, he'd sorted out the logistics of her problems and not wanted to delve into the emotional side. While Toni had been supportive in every way. She might've always run to Greyson, knowing that Toni was always two steps away ready to catch her before she fell. And that was why, as she'd gotten older, she'd kept Toni at a safe distance. He was a risk her heart couldn't take. Until now.

But somehow, she didn't think he'd had becoming a parent in mind.

Well, if anything, she'd get her closure with Greyson. He was going to be the uncle to their baby after all.

When she finally arrived, the house was in darkness. *He works in a restaurant. Why would he be here?* Not everybody stayed home with their families at Christmas. Plenty didn't even celebrate the holiday. She had a long wait ahead.

She'd already waited hours to get a flight. What was a few extra?

Brownstones lined each side of the street. Trees were dotted along the pavement, caged in wrought iron. Here, nature was corralled and controlled. Pruned to fit into human ideals of conformity to beauty. She preferred the wild open. She never could have fitted in. On some level, Grey must have known that.

Huddled on the stoop, she rested her chin on her knees, and raised her hood over her head. Fatigue infiltrated her flesh. She was unable to keep it at bay any longer. Her eyelids drooped. The streetscape blurred like a painting by Monet. Occasionally a passing car would draw her mind out of the haze.

What seemed like hours later, headlights washed across the snow-encrusted ground. She lifted her head, squinting against the intrusion. Recognizing Greyson's truck, she pulled her stiff body to a stand.

He got out and approached her. "Lory? For Christ's sake, you'll catch your death. Come here."

Picking her up in a bear hug, he put her in his truck and covered her with a blanket. Heated air blasted from the vents coaxing her towards it.

"What are you doing here?" He pushed a button on a clicker and the garage door began to open.

"Merry Christmas to you too, Grey." She didn't realize how cold she'd been until she spoke, and her teeth clacked together.

"Sorry, *topolina*. Merry Christmas. How long have you been sitting there? Why didn't you tell me you were coming? Why aren't you home with your family?" He parked the car but left the engine running.

She used to love it when he called her little mouse. The endearment didn't have the same effect on her now. He looked the same. Long, dark hair. His face so much like his brother's. There was something in his eyes though. A flicker of light she'd never seen.

There was one major difference. For all the times she'd sat in that very seat next to him, this was the first time he didn't give her butterflies. The dynamic between them was calmer. More balanced.

The way it should have been all along.

She checked her phone, ignoring the notifications lined up on the screen. "An hour or so. I wanted to see you."

"Is everything okay?"

Lord help me. I've screwed up. She pushed her hood off her head. "Oh, yeah. It's fine. Fine."

"Uh-huh. Totally convincing. Let's get into the warm house, and you can tell me what's going on." He led her through the house to the living area upstairs. *Wow.* The place was lush. Designer everything. What it lacked was character. Color. Life.

She placed her bag on a chair by the fireplace and discarded her phone on the coffee table. It was nearly midnight in Boston and she had three missed calls from Toni, two from Clay, and more from her mama.

"The bathroom is through there. I'll light the fire and make us some hot chocolate. We've got Christmas pudding somewhere too. Would you like a slice?"

The mere thought of the rich foods had nausea punching her insides. She fixated on the bathroom door as she spoke. "Could I just have some tea and crackers? I don't know if I can stomach anything heavy at the moment."

"Yeah, sure. We should have some tea."

She heard a question in his voice, but she was already busting through the door.

She made sure to clip the lock before kneeling in front of the toilet. She tossed off her coat. Sweat beaded on her brow. If she'd been freezing before, she was boiling now. Her breath sawed in and out. Naming it 'morning' sickness was someone's cruel joke. This baby had hijacked her body and her life. For all her initial denial and resistance, she'd come to a place where she gave in willingly. She was going to be a mama. She'd done enough research in the last week to figure out she was about two months along. That meant it had happened on the night after the fair. Their first time.

Her stomach heaved and she coughed up the water she'd drunk at the airport. She retched until there was nothing left and then she retched some more.

There was a tap on the door. "Lory? Are you okay in there?"

"Be—" Her stomach attempted another evac. "Be there in a minute."

"Are you sick?"

Kinda. The door handle jiggled.

Oh, Jesus, Grey. Do not *open that door.*

Thankfully, his footsteps retreated, and her stomach finally settled. She flushed, washed her hands and face, and headed for a seat beside the fire. Grey was in the kitchen. Two steaming mugs sat on the counter.

"Sorry. It's been a long day. I guess it all caught up to me." *I have to tell him.*

"That's okay. You had me worried." He made his way over with their drinks. A plate of crackers already sat on the sofa across from her.

She tugged on her sweater, wondering if he noticed how loose it was compared to the last time he'd seen her wear it. "Thanks." She took the cup from him.

"Do I need to ask again?"

"I'm pregnant." *Ta da.*

"You're what?"

You heard correctly. "Preg. Nant."

The way his surprise mirrored his brother's was darkly comical. It was like going through the whole thing again. She would have laughed if she had the energy. Except Toni's surprise had rapidly morphed into sheer terror. The chill returned, and she curled her hands around the warm beverage, blowing the steam.

Grey seemed confused; grooves etched between his brows.

And then his eyes narrowed. His fists clenched before he shot to his feet. "I'm gonna kill him."

Who does he think the father is? "Kill who, Grey? Sit down. It's midnight on Christmas Day."

He always did have a quick temper. Toni's was more of a simmer than a flare.

"Jake Johnson. That sonofabitch."

She almost laughed. What was it with Jake and the Agrioli men? He'd never held any appeal for her. "It's not his."

Grey seemed to deflate, falling onto the sofa. "Who, then?"

She stared into her mug, not wanting to see his face when she dropped this particular nugget of info. "Toni. Toni is the father."

"Toni? As in, Antonio? My brother, Antonio?"

Her eyes flicked to his briefly before detouring to the flickering flames.

"I told him to look after you, not climb on top of you. Holy hell." He performed the same move his brother had done when she'd told him the news— cradled his head and dragged his hands down his neck like he wanted to pull the skin from his flesh. She stiffened as the déjà vu gripped her by the throat.

"Does anyone else know?"

She pulled in a breath before answering with a smirk. "Toni knows."

"How did he take the news?"

"The same way you did, but with shorter hair."

His hands bounced on his thighs as he dropped them. "Sorry. It's a shock. He can't have been too surprised. He was there when it happened."

You're kidding, right? He said it as if he thought they'd planned this. And even if they had, was anyone not bewildered at the reality of facing a complete life one eighty? But Toni had been more than astonished. He'd been horrified.

She cleared her throat. "I was on the pill. We were careful." Her grip on the cup tightened as memories of that night came rushing back. They'd been phenomenal together. Apart from the condom, there'd been nothing careful about it. Instinctual, primal, carnal. . . not careful. This baby had been made with love.

"So, it was an accident?" His eyebrows raised.

She remembered watching the second line appear on the pregnancy test. *Accident* sounded so wrong. "Neither of us thought it would actually happen."

"Well, it has. So, what's he gonna do about it?"

Her eyes narrowed. *Jesus.* Like the baby was a problem to be solved? Toni's problem. "What do you mean, 'what's he gonna do about it?' I'm the pregnant one—not him."

"He might not be carrying the bun, but he's responsible for putting it there, and he damn well better look after you while it bakes. I can't believe he let you travel in your state. Have you been eating at all? Your family must've noticed."

The machine gun delivery of judgements and questions ticked her off. "I've been busy elsewhere at mealtimes. Toni doesn't know I'm here."

"You just took off?" Grey crossed his arms.

Well, now she had an attack of the guilts. "Kinda, yeah. I told Clay I was coming to surprise you. Toni probably knows by now." She could only imagine how he might be handling the situation. Maybe he'd recovered from the jolt and he was ready to talk? Maybe she'd ring him in the morning?

Why did I run away?

On the coffee table, her phone lit up with Antonio's number.

"It's him," she croaked, eyes flooding with tears.

I can't.

"I'll handle it. You drink your tea. There's a spare room—second door on the left up the stairs. Help yourself. It's late."

Maybe it was cowardly, but she grabbed her drink like it was her safety blanket and hotfooted it up the stairs. Not quick enough to miss Grey's greeting for his brother, though.

"What the fuck have you done?"

Nice, Grey.

She clicked the door closed, kicked off her boots, and got under the warm bed covers.

Antonio hadn't been the only one involved. It took two to create a life.

Wasn't that the crux of the problem?

It takes two to make a life together.

Was she going to have to raise this child on her own?

———

She tiptoed downstairs the next morning, not wanting to wake anyone. It was barely six, but her bladder and her stomach woke her up, both wanting to empty their contents. If she could find where they kept the crackers, she'd be okay.

"Mornin'." Grey's voice cut through the quiet.

"Shit!" Startled, she grabbed for the banister.

"Sorry." He grinned. "I heard you get up. Did you sleep well?"

"A bit." She made her way into the kitchen, noting that he'd lit the fire.

"Do you want crackers?"

"Yes, please."

He pushed a plate across the stone benchtop. "How about some tea to go with them?"

Taking a seat on one of the stools at the island bench, she reached for the food. "Actually, do you have juice?"

"Cranberry."

"That'll do. Thanks." She nibbled on a cracker, appreciating its bland taste. "Was Toni okay?"

"He was ready to come and get you."

"What?" The half-eaten snack dangled from her fingers.

"Don't worry; he's not comin'."

"I've gotta go back, anyways. It was stupid of me to run."

He leaned on his elbows, meeting her stare. "I'm glad you came. But I'm surprised you chose to come here."

"I wasn't thinking."

Grey winced, pushing back to stand and gripping the edge of the bench. "Ouch. I deserved that. And I never said how sorry I was. I shouldn't have run out on ya like that."

"You hurt me." The remnants of the pain niggled behind her sternum before fading away.

It was funny; she'd spent weeks going over and over so many questions in her mind. If she'd had the chance to confront him, she would've unleashed them all one by one.

What could she have done to make him stay?

Why wasn't she good enough?

Why didn't he ask her to go with him?

What mistakes had she made?

The answers were all so clear to her now, she didn't need to ask.

She was worthy. She hadn't done anything wrong. There was nothing she could've said to make him stay, because nobody could *make* anyone love them. Her and Greyson weren't meant to be.

It didn't hurt anymore. She was so thankful she didn't get what she thought she wanted.

"You had to. I see that now. You set me free to find a greater love."

Even if things didn't work out with Toni, she deserved a deep, messy kind of love that consumed her whole and nourished her soul. "We would have been happy enough, but there was something missing. It would have festered into resentment eventually. And I wouldn't want that for us. I care about you. A lot. I still love you. As my friend. As family." The words spilled like a release. A final snapping of a cord that had frayed over time.

He dropped his gaze. "You are so much better than me. I never deserved you. I am sorry."

"It's okay. Time to leave it in the past." She reached across the counter, clasping his hand in hers. "What about you? Is there anyone special?"

"Would you be angry if I said yes?" He watched her through his lashes.

She barked out a laugh. "I'm pregnant with your brother's child. I think it's safe to say I have no right to be upset if you've moved on."

His eyes widened as if something had just occurred to him. "I'm gonna be an uncle."

Lory's face split in a toothy smile. "Yup."

And I'm gonna be a mama.

"So, what's her name?"

"Chelsea," his voice caressed the word with adoration.

It was good to see him happy.

"Tell me all about her."

Chapter FOURTEEN

Merry Christmas

Antonio

"Thanks for giving me a lift to the airport." Anton adjusted his seatbelt. He figured Clay would have questions that he wasn't ready to answer. *Fuck it.* Lory had left her car in Jackson, and Anton didn't want her driving all the way back on her own. Plus, he wanted to see her the minute she set foot on Mississippi soil. So he needed Clay's help.

"No problem. You wanna tell me what's going on?"

Nope. But you're gonna find out anyways. "Lory and I have been dating for a few months."

Clay's jaw stretched. "It's nice to finally be told the truth."

So, they had been found out. "I wanted us on solid ground before everyone could put their opinions in the pot."

"I get it." He nodded once. "It's a little soon, don't you think? And with you being the ex's brother, it's kinda hard to wrap my head around it."

"I've waited decades for her." If he was going to spill the truth, he was gonna let out the whole shebang.

Clay's eyes bulged. "Whoa! What?"

"And she finally sees me as more than a friend."

"Shut the farmhouse door!" His mouth gaped as he stared at the road ahead. "Why'd she run off to him, then?"

"I wish I knew. My guess is that she's scared shitless of becoming a mother."

"Huh?" His head whipped sideways.

Oh good, you are paying attention. "She's pregnant."

"What the fuck?" he roared. The wheel wobbled before he regained control. "Jesus, you tell me this while I'm going sixty-five on the highway. I oughta pull over and deck you."

Go for it. I deserve it. "Do what you want. Just get me there on time. I don't want her waiting."

Clay's head swiveled back and forth between the road and Antonio. "You really love her, don't ya?"

More than I thought was possible. "I have for decades."

"Well, shit." He slapped a hand on his thigh. "Why did you hide it?"

Anton shrugged. "She was with Grey. What could I do?"

"Man, that must've killed you."

Anton focused ahead, not wanting to drag that agony out of storage. Not until he saw her.

"Yeah, I wouldn't wanna go there either. This is why I ain't lookin' for love. All it brings is pain."

"The pain is worth it."

"You can believe that all you want, but I ain't buyin' it." Clay flicked on his blinker to pass a minivan.

Poor, naïve shmuck. "Yeah, good luck with that, Clay. You can run, but you can't hide. If it finds you, you got no choice but to succumb."

"Sounds like a goddamn disease."

In a way, it was. It had altered him forever. The only cure was to nurture it and let it take over.

"I guess congrats are in order, brother." Clay bumped fists with Anton.

"Thanks." He nodded, smiling.

"I won't stick around when we get there. I don't wanna see all that mushy shit. You guys have stuff to sort out, and I've got leftover turducken to eat. You okay with that?"

"I appreciate it."

———

He waited in the arrivals hall at Jackson Evers International, keeping an eye on the gate where she'd be disembarking. Greyson had finally done something right and texted Anton her flight number after seeing her safely to the airport.

He saw her hair first. She had it tied in a high ponytail. Her bloodshot eyes and slow gait cooled his anger. She trudged along like she had nothing left in the tank. His protective instincts kicked in. He thought about gathering her in his arms and carrying her to the car. Maybe she wouldn't appreciate him making a scene. He didn't particularly give a shit what anyone else thought.

With her eyes down, she didn't see him until he blocked her path. She pulled up short. "What are you doing here?"

"Picking you up." He fought the craving to hold her.

"You didn't have to do that."

Slipping his hand into hers, he pulled her out of the flow of bodies heading for the doors. "Are you kidding?"

Her mouth drew down, her lids drifting shut. "I don't want to fight."

After finding a row of empty seats, he guided her there to rest. "I'm not fighting. I'm just amazed that you'd think I wouldn't want to be here when you got back."

"You weren't happy the last time I saw you," she mumbled.

He folded his arms, releasing a sigh, wanting to peel off his skin again but this time for the way he'd reacted to the news. "I was blindsided, Lory. Cut me some slack."

"We're arguing."

And they were drawing a crowd, rubberneckers slowing to eavesdrop. "We have a lot to say to each other. Can I have the keys, please?"

She pulled them out of her pocketbook and slapped them in his open palm.

He took her backpack, too. "Ready?"

She pouted.

He cradled her face and kissed her deep. "It's damn good to see you."

Tears were poised in the corners of her eyes, ready to spill.

He tugged her hand, wanting to get out of there ASAP. "Where are you parked?"

"Follow me." She eased to her feet and led him to the exit.

Ten minutes later, they were pulling out of the airport and heading into town.

"You missed the turnoff." Lory's head twisted as she pointed at the side road heading south.

"Yep."

"We're not going home?"

"Nope. I booked us a room at The Fairview Inn."

A huge smile overtook her face. "Really?"

"Really."

Her dimpled grin was worth every penny.

He rested his hand on her thigh for the remainder of the ride, needing the contact and the reassurance that she was there with him.

He took pleasure in the fact that she leaned forward as the inn came into view, her eyes staring in wonder. The sprawling white building with its proud columns and French windows oozed class while keeping true to its historical significance.

Knowing she was tired, Anton hustled to check in before finding their room and opening the door for her to enter.

"Oh, wow. It's beautiful," she cooed.

Yes, it was. A carved wooden bed invited them to stay the night. In the corner, a reading nook featured a black leather wingback chair, daring any booklover to resist its charm. And the kicker—an open fireplace.

Damn, I'm good.

"Why don't you have a shower while I light the fire?" He took off his jacket.

"You don't have to tell me twice." She stripped off her coat and boots before disappearing into the bathroom.

He stacked the kindling, waiting for it to catch before adding the larger pieces. It was crackling nicely by the time she emerged wearing the complimentary robe.

"Are you having one?"

"I showered before I left." He sidled over to her, scooped his arms behind her back and knees, and lifted her in his hold.

She shrieked, grabbing his shoulders.

"Screamer." Pecking her on the mouth, he deposited her on the bed. "Do you need to eat? Drink?"

"I could use some water."

After searching the bar fridge, he found a bottle and handed it to her.

"Thank you."

Lying beside her, he propped himself up on one elbow. The lump that had been trapped in his throat since she'd left, layered his tongue with gravity. "Why'd you go runnin' off to Grey?" He focused on the pulse in her neck, unable to meet her eyes. "Am I just a consolation prize? Do you still feel somethin' for him?"

Her hands flew to cover her face. "No! I knew it was stupid the minute I got there. Before I'd even seen him," she groaned as she slapped her hands on the bed. "I'm sorry. I shouldn't have gone."

His lungs deflated. *Thank fuck.* Tension seeped out of his shoulders and he flopped his head onto the pillow. Could he really blame her for wanting to get away from him after his catatonic response? Especially since he'd stupidly been keeping their relationship under wraps? "I'm sorry, too." The fire hissed and popped as the silence between them stretched. He searched her eyes, finding remorse and a whole lot of love. "I forgive you. Please don't do it again."

"I won't. What I felt for him was infatuation. I looked to him as my guide because he always made the decisions."

"You don't need anyone to choose for you."

"I know."

"But when something involves the both of us…" He spread his fingers over her belly. "…the three of us, we need to sort it out together."

She nodded, placing her hand on top of his.

Curling on her side, she wrapped an arm around his back, and spoke into his chest. "You won't leave me, will you, Toni?"

"Is that what you thought? That I would knock you up and abandon you to go it alone?"

Her eyes slid away, as her cheeks flushed. "It sounds stupid when *you* say it."

Oh, silly girl. He pressed his lips into her hair, breathing in her sweet apple scent. A balm to the jealousy he harbored towards his brother. A shot of adrenaline to speed up his heart. "No, sweetheart. Never." *I will never be able to tear myself away from you.* "Now might be a good time to give you your Christmas present."

"I forgot! Merry Christmas for yesterday." She stretched for a kiss.

"Wait." He left her for a moment to dig through his jacket pocket and hid the gift behind his back before resuming his position. "Merry Christmas." He placed the velvet box in her palm, watching her eyes peel wide as she opened it. "Marry me?"

Jaw dropping, her breath rushed out. "Is this the present you bought last week?"

"Yeah."

"But. . . isn't it too soon?" She gnawed on her bottom lip, worry creasing her brow.

"Time has nothin' to do with it. When you know, you know. Unless. . . *you* don't." He resisted a smirk, his heart full with confidence that she was all his.

"What? Yes! Yes, I do. I will. Are you kidding?"

"Not about something so important, no." Now, he did smirk.

She rolled her eyes. "Ugh, you drive me nuts. Shut up and kiss me."

No problem, sweetheart. He kissed the living heck out of her. All over her body, giving special attention to her stomach… and lower.

He had her naked in the firelight for the second time.

It was beginning to be his favorite thing.

Chapter FIFTEEN

History Repeats (Kinda)

Antonio

Anton opened the passenger door of his truck, guiding his fiancée to the farmhouse door. Checking his watch, he confirmed it was lunchtime. The delicious aroma wafting on the breeze agreed. Who needed a dinner bell when they had Nonna's cooking?

With their hands clasped, the cool metal band of Lory's engagement ring rested against his finger, inflating his chest with pride. She was finally his. He bent to give her a peck on the forehead. "Are you ready for this?"

"Do you think they'll be mad?" She tightened her grip.

"This will be the first grandchild. They'll be stoked." *Or not.* They might be pissed. He didn't really give a shit. *Time to find out.*

"Not just about the baby. I mean about us." Her voice faded as the corners of her mouth turned down.

"They know I went to pick you up from the airport and that we've spent the night together. I think they've figured it out by now. Besides, I don't care what they think. It's nobody's business but ours. And if they really love us, they want us to be happy."

He pushed through the entrance, going straight to the kitchen. Five pairs of eyes locked onto his. His sisters stared, both holding pieces of bread in identical poses. Nonna winked, flashing her dentures. Papà's features relaxed into a mask of indifference.

Mama came towards them with open arms. "Everything okay?" She caught them in a group hug.

"*Sì.*" He nodded.

She lifted Lory's chin and gave her a reassuring smile. "I'm glad you're back."

Lory's gaze slid sideways to Antonio as she bit her lip.

It's okay. He slipped an arm across her shoulders. "We have something to tell you."

Mama tensed before stepping away. "Is Grey alright?"

"Oh, he's doing fine." Lory spoke up.

"We're engaged and Lory's going to have our baby." *May as well get it all out.*

The pieces of bread dropped from his sisters' hands with perfectly synchronized thuds. His papa leaned back in his chair, smirking. Nonna grinned from ear to ear, resting her chin on her palm.

Mama opened and closed her mouth a few times before saying, "No!"

Okay, whoa. Role reversal. That was supposed to be Papà's line. "Excuse me?"

"No. This can't be happening again." She shook her head so hard, hair loosened from her bun.

Lorelei leaned into his side, turning her face to the floor.

For the first time, he was angry at his mother. Pressure welled behind his sternum and he forced it from his mouth. "Mama!"

"Nelle. *Sedere.*" Papà's bark stopped Anton from saying anymore.

His mother fell into her chair, obeying the command to sit.

"You, too." Papà waggled a finger in Anton and Lory's direction. "I have a story to tell. It's time we cleared the air."

Anton pulled out a seat for Lory before taking his beside her. *What the hell is going on?* His mama had been acting weird at the show. Maybe this had something to do with her behavior? He tried to relax his jaw as he focused on his father.

Papà pushed his plate aside and clasped his hands on the table. "Your uncle and I met your mother at the sale yards when we were teenagers. I'd never seen anyone so beautiful in my life." He pulled Mama's hand into his, giving it a kiss. Tears streamed down her face as she blinked at him. "I didn't see her for weeks afterwards. Not until she walked in here with Matteo."

Holy shit. She'd been with his uncle. *Oh... ooooooh.*

"Oh, my God," Marianne gasped.

Nonna slapped a palm on the table, shushing her.

For once, Sophia was speechless.

Papà cleared his throat. "When I told you, *a father knows his son*, I meant it. I know you because I was in the same position as you. I loved your mother from afar for years, hoping that one day she would see that she was the center of my world." He tapped a finger on his temple. "And she did. Matteo never put her first."

"So, she figured it out and you got your happy ever after." Anton raised his brows and turned to his mother. "Why are you upset about me and Lory?"

"I'm sorry. My outburst was uncalled for. I am happy for you both. And extremely pleased that Lory will officially be a part of our family." The words came out in a rush as she stared at the table in front of her.

Anton shook his head, brow bunched in confusion. "None of that explains your reaction."

Her shoulders rose as she drew in a breath. "Matteo left me in pieces when he told me of his plans to leave. Your father put me back together. I found out I was pregnant not too long after your uncle left."

"Okay." *So what?* He swiveled his head, looking between his parents for some clue to the problem.

"We don't know who Greyson's biological father is," Mama croaked.

Holy fuck! That's a big ass skeleton you've been hiding.

"*Basta*!" *Enough!* "We don't need to know. He's my son." One heavy finger just about drilled through the table to emphasize his point. Papà pushed his chair back before standing tall. "Back to work." He squeezed Antonio's shoulder on his way past. A *congratulations*, Papà style.

At his command, Nonna and his daughters made themselves scarce. Anton and Lory were left to stare at his distraught mother. The three of them sat in silence for an interminably long time, the ticking of the clock there to mark the barrage of emotions tumbling across the wooden surface from Mama's side of the table.

Lory moved to take a seat beside her, offering comfort in an embrace.

He leaned back, processing the drama exposé. All this time she'd carried this secret. His father didn't seem to care. In a way, Anton understood. Papà had raised Grey as his own. It took more than one sperm to make a man a father. What if a test showed that he wasn't? That would be devastating. Was he better off believing Grey was his biological son without concrete evidence?

Would I want to know?

Yeah. Yeah, I would.

"Why don't you find out?"

Mama's head popped up and she wiped her face. "I intend to." Her shoulders rose as she sucked in some air. She met Anton's assessing stare with a smile. "But first, I'm going to organize a baby shower and an engagement party." Giving Lory one last hug before rounding the table to give Anton the same, she added, "I love you. Congratulations."

"Love you too, Mama."

Epilogue

Antonio

July

Lory cradled, Jack Lucca Clay Agrioli as he suckled at her breast. The sun streamed in through the venetians, playing patterns across her bare skin. Anton lounged in the recliner beside the hospital bed, fascinated by the sight of his new family. Lorelei was a natural. He could not have wished for more.

"He's asleep. Can you put him in the crib for me?"

She covered her chest and passed Anton the precious bundle. He was careful not to jostle Jack as he placed him down with the precision of a bomb expert.

There was a soft knock at the door.

Goddamn it. Every time. "Whoever that is, they better not wake him up," He mumbled under his breath as he opened the barrier to find his brother peering through a bunch of flowers.

Anton placed his finger over his mouth in warning before he went in for a hug.

They both padded into the room, Grey handing the bouquet to Anton to sort out. He grabbed a vase to put the flowers in, placing it on the nightstand.

Lory's face lifted into a tired smile. "Hi stranger."

Grey kissed her on the cheek before peering into the cradle. "Looks like an Agrioli. All that black hair. You did good. How are you doing, *topolina*?"

"I'm okay. Exhausted. Happy. Sore."

Grey shoved his hands in his back pockets. "I bet. I won't stay long. I went to visit the farmhouse. The proud grandparents told me the news."

"What are you doing in Mississippi?" Anton took a seat on the bed. Resisting a smirk, he remembered their trip to Boston only a couple of months ago. Lory and he had met Grey's girlfriend. Scared her off, more like it. Grey had his work cut out for him there.

Big brother had finally met his match.

Grey rocked on his heels, like he wanted out of there already. "I quit my apprenticeship."

"What?" Lory's eyes bugged.

"Yeah. Boston wasn't for me."

Huh. Chelsea must have left. Only a woman would be able to convince his pigheaded brother to alter his plans. Anton leaned his elbows on the bed. "So, you're moving back permanently?"

"No. I'm heading east to Bama."

"Chelsea?" Anton and Lory asked in sync.

Grey dipped his chin. "Chelsea."

Anton grinned. *I knew it.* "How did Uncle Matteo take the news?"

Screwing up his nose, Grey shook his head. "He'll get over it. I hope he comes to visit soon. Him and Papà need to kiss and make up."

"It's hard for Matteo." *Poor bastard.* "Mama chose to be with Papà before Matteo decided to go. He left here broken-hearted."

"Yeah, well the restaurant is his mistress now. His pride was hurt more than his heart." Crossing his arms, Grey shrugged.

"Maybe so. At least Mama knows who her baby daddy is now."

"Twenty-five years later." Grey rolled his eyes. "She chose the right brother."

Anton turned to Lory, giving her a wink.

Yes, she did.

True love always finds its way.

Home, sweet home.

Acknowledgements

Writing a book in 2020 has been a phenomenal challenge. Particularly a romance. It would have been so much easier to write a horror. And still, I must thank all the fans of this series for bringing me back to contemporary romance. After a couple of years writing paranormal/ supernatural storylines, it was a welcome change and a much-needed distraction.

I sincerely hope that you and your loved ones are navigating your way through this new paradigm with minimal disruption. But the reality is, this year has been FUBAR (any fans of *Saving Private Ryan* out there?) Thank God for books. Thank goodness for movies, art, poetry, and music. Thank the heavens for the great outdoors and for people with big hearts who reach out to lend a hand where it's needed. Please ask someone for help if you're struggling. You are never alone. Ever.

So much love to all my readers who continue to support me. To those who go the extra mile (you know who you are) and share, like, subscribe, comment and interact in any form, I send an enormous thanks for all the love.

My betas—Lisa and Kat—huge thanks for your valued input.

To Bec, who reads every, last word, a special dose of gratitude goes out to you.

All my lovely Gems in my reader group, you have no idea how much you inspire me to keep going.

And finally, to every wonderful person who volunteered to read the advanced copy and/or drop a review—love, love, love to you.

Brittany from Off the Book Pages, you are amazing, woman! Thank you for being such a huge support of indie authors around the globe!

The beautiful souls at Creating Ink suffered through reading a truly awful rough draft and managed to steer me in the right direction. I can't thank you enough for your patience and guidance.

Fiona, you managed to squeeze me into your proofing schedule again! Mwah.

My boys… I can't imagine life without you. Thank you for understanding when I need to disappear into my writing cave. You are my heart.

Thanks to my beautiful friends and family whose support is an unsinkable life raft, and a priceless treasure. Can you feel the bear hug? Yeah, you can.

Thank you!

Read on for an excerpt from Finding Home.

Excerpt from finding HOME

Chapter One

Hard Decisions

2006

Greyson's lungs convulsed from sucking down too much dust, diesel fumes, and cow stench, as he tossed another hay bale onto the truck. Bending forward, he spat the grit from his mouth, watching his shadow jerk as he returned a little piece of Mississippi to its rightful place.

"Fuck this shit."

The muffled protest came out of his mouth once a week, probably closer to daily in the last few weeks, as his desperation became a palpable force driving him to crazy town.

Wiping his mouth on his shoulder, he walked behind the rumbling truck, inching its way around the loose bales in the field.

"Shut up before Papà hears you."

Turning his head, Grey leveled a sneer at his brother for daring to scold him. "He won't hear, he's driving the truck. Besides, I don't give a shit if he hears. I hate this job and he knows it."

"He might know it, but he won't accept it."

Antonio threw another bale and straightened with a groan. Removing one worn leather glove and his hat, he scrubbed a hand over his sweaty buzz cut. It was clear they were brothers in the same dark shade of their hair, their slate gray eyes, and strong chins. A legacy from their father and his Italian heritage. But their differing hair styles were the clearest indicator of their personalities. Antonio was happy to conform, while Grey's hair hadn't seen the clippers for four years. He had no interest in fitting into anyone's regulations. The ponytail he wore was a big *fuck you* to conformity.

"He'll have to accept it soon enough."

Removing his cowboy hat, Grey tugged on the ends of his hair, dislodging the piece of hay that was scratching under his collar.

"What are you talkin' about?" Anton flicked his eyes sidelong, taking a swig from his water bottle.

Plonking his hat back on his head, Greyson grabbed his own bottle. "I'm leavin'." He stared down his brother, challenge marking his face and his stance.

"What are you talkin' about? Where are you goin'?" The water bottle dangled from lax fingers, all but forgotten, as Anton gaped at his older brother.

"You repeat yourself a lot. You know that?" Grey smirked.

"Cut the shit, Grey. Where are you going? Does Mama know?"

"She's been supportive."

He bent, heaving another bale through the air to be caught and stacked on the truck by the ranch hands. His two sisters were taking turns walking beside the vehicle, guiding Papà when to stop or slow down.

"She wants me to follow my heart."

"Where to?" Shock lifted the pitch of Antonio's voice.

"The kitchen. A real kitchen where I can learn to cook from the best."

"You're not serious?" Capping his bottle and letting out a shrill whistle, Anton threw it to one of the ranch hands on the truck. "He'll never speak to you again. You know what happened to our uncle."

Yeah, success happened. If his father couldn't support that, then… Grey didn't give a fuck.

The bitter fallout from Uncle Matteo's escape still lingered in the old farmhouse. A constant pollution of ash in the air, cloying every conversation or family gathering where his absence was glaringly obvious.

Greyson clenched gloved fists, holding his body in check. He didn't want to antagonize his brother. Antonio was built for ranch life. Grey wasn't.

"I'm aware, and I'm willing to take the chance. It's worth it. I can't rot away on this ranch. It's not the life I want."

"What about the family?" Anton's arms flailed, emphasizing his point. "What about your friends? Lory?"

"Lory would want me to be happy."

His younger brother took off his hat, slapped it on his thigh, and whistled a long, low note. He eyeballed Grey under heavy brows, shaking his head. "You haven't told her. You're a chicken shit."

Grey's muscles tightened, gathering for a fight.

One side of Anton's mouth tipped up in a mocking smile. "Well… I'll miss ya. I'd say make sure you visit, but I don't know if you'll be welcome."

The tension seeped out a little, but Grey knew it wouldn't disappear until he was in his pickup on the interstate.

"I'll visit anyway. He can't stop me from coming to town."

"*Basta*!" The brothers whipped their heads toward the truck where their father was leaning out of the window, motioning with his arm. "When you're done with your women's meeting, maybe you could load the truck."

"*Sì*, Papà." Antonio tipped his chin in acknowledgement before turning back to Grey. "Come on. Let's get this done so we can enjoy some of Nonna's pasta."

Eyeing the back of his papà's head through narrowed slits, the muscles in Grey's jaw worked out his annoyance. He'd grind his teeth to stumps if he stayed here any longer. Shifting his gaze, he watched his brother diligently working at clearing all the bales. He didn't seem all that concerned about Grey leaving. Or maybe he didn't believe that Grey would go through with it.

His determination solidified. He could no longer spend his life doing something he didn't care for. He was already half packed. It was only a matter of days. All he had to do was tell his papà.

They finally finished loading the last of about two thousand bales. Garlic wafted down the dust track and over their makeshift seats of hay, as they made their way back to the hay barn. He could see the old white farmhouse in the distance, with its dormer windows marking the second story bedrooms, and the long veranda where he'd often sit listening to the sounds of the night.

Grey's nose twitched, capturing the alluring scent. Way better than cow shit, or almost anything he could think of. He rubbed his callused palms together, thinking about going into the kitchen after they off-loaded the bales. It was a distraction from the nerves rampaging in his stomach at the thought of the conversation that had to happen soon. If he was smart, he'd let it wait until his father was full-bellied after a hearty meal.

Grey jumped down, listening to his papà's barrage of instructions, as if they all didn't know how to operate the bale elevator, or stack hay. They'd been doing this for years, for Christ's sake. Every word from that man's mouth was gasoline on the fire in Grey's belly to get the hell out. Every muscle ache, every creak in his bones, every scratch or cut on his skin, drove the flames higher.

He stretched his neck, pinched his mouth shut, and took up his position at the elevator, ready to unload his last bales of hay. If he never saw hay again, he'd be as happy as… a chef in a kitchen.

Want to keep reading the rest of the story? Find it at jmadele.org.

About the AUTHOR

Author of smart, sexy characters, J.M. Adele loves to flit between the dark and light sides of romance. Somewhere along the way an almost constant procession of imaginary characters settled into her thoughts and she picked up a pen to share their stories.

She lives in Queensland with her three greatest loves, her children. When she's not writing or being a mum, you might find her hiking up a mountain, singing in the car when nobody is looking, or curled up with a good book.

Get updates about new releases, sales, and exclusive
tidbits by joining my newsletter.
Head to my website to find out more.
Oh, and you get a free book too!

jmadele.org

https://www.facebook.com/authorjmadele

https://twitter.com/JMAdeleBooks

https://www.instagram.com/j.m.adele/

https://www.pinterest.com.au/jmadele/_created/